I0645615

Laughing At Shadows

Edited by Brett Reistroffer

A collection of funny, dark, and weird horror stories for funny, dark, and weird people.

Anthology Copyright 2020

Copyrights to the individual works contained in this collection belong to the credited authors:

Murder Sandwich ©2020 Skyler Goff; *Overdue Notice* ©2020 Andrew Johnston; *Bad Dates and Dragons* ©2020 Alyssa Eckles; *The Haunting of Peruvius Corcorant* ©2020 George Nikolopoulos; *It Came From Mail Order* ©2020 Eric J. Guignard; *Captain Pistachio's Charming Rampage* ©2020 Jeff Strand; *Your Diabolical Baby* ©2020 (English) Santiago Eximeno; *The Night Stockers* ©2020 Sean Logan; *Dying Art* ©2020 C L Raven; *Tea Time* ©2020 William West; *All Aboard!* ©2020 Brandon Butler; *Vlad's Incorruptible Soul* ©2020 W. T. Paterson

Edited by Brett Reistroffer

Printed in the United States of America

First Edition: 2020

eBook ISBN 978-0-9960381-8-8

Softcover ISBN 978-0-9960381-6-4

Published By Bad Dream Entertainment®

www.BadDreamEntertainment.com

Cover Illustration by Stefan Koidl

Graphic Design by Rogues Hollow Productions

Final Manuscript Polish by Mellisa Peitsch

The 'EyeBrain' logo is a registered trademark of Bad Dream Entertainment, Seattle, WA.

Original trademark design by Darcray

For anyone who laughs in the theater while everyone else is screaming.

Table of Contents

Introduction

By editor Brett Reistroffer

There is plenty to be said about the relationship between horror and humor. Even though they are seemingly on opposite sides of the emotional spectrum, the two are often inseparable. It's tempting to wax on about how humor acts as a natural release valve for the anxiety of horror, or how they are both merely different ways to process the absurdities of the human condition, but there are people much more qualified and capable than I to tackle the deep thinking on the subject. Besides, you picked up this collection of stories for a good chuckle, a quick scare, or merely to pass some time at the bus stop, not to listen to some hack who gets to call himself an editor because he somehow convinced a bunch of talented writers to let him publish their stories (hint: it was money).

The one thing I will say is that if this anthology has a single purpose it's to have fun, because that's really why we're all in the spooky business to begin with, regardless of how serious we sometimes like to take this genre we call horror, as outlandish as it often is. So read on and enjoy stories of vengeful vegans, psychotic seahorses, and homicidal pistachios; just have some fun while doing it and remember that a good scare can be just as ridiculous as a good joke. After all, you can't spell slaughter without laughter.

Brett R,

July 2019

Murder Sandwich

Skyler Goff

Whisper Meadows woke to the sweet smell of fried ham and promptly vomited.

"Danny!" she shouted through a mouth of acid and bile. "What the hell? Are you really cooking ham?" She and Danny had been in an open relationship for over three years and he knew damn well that she didn't allow animal flesh or byproduct in their apartment.

But she wasn't in their apartment.

She was on a cot in a cell surrounded by bars on two of its four sides, the other two sides thick, graffitied concrete. A single bulb hung over a table and chair.

On the table was a ham sandwich on a ceramic plate.

Whisper began to scream.

A click. The sound of feedback. A voice spoke to her.

"Whisper." The voice was distorted just like those of protected witnesses on the crime shows Whisper's father had made her watch when she lived back home. "Such an ironic name for someone so loud."

"Why the hell is there a ham sandwich in here with me?" Whisper screamed. "Get it away from me!"

"You—" The voice went silent for a second and then came back, the vicious edge turned into confusion. "You want me to get rid of the sandwich?"

"Yes! God!" Whisper sobbed. "I'm a vegan. Animal flesh makes me physically ill!"

Another pause.

"Do—do you know that you're chained to the wall?"

Whisper looked down at her ankle and saw that she was, in fact, chained to the wall.

"Are you going to get rid of the sandwich or not?" she called out.

"You aren't going to eat it?"

"I'm not touching that murder sandwich. No way."

Silence.

"I said," Whisper shouted through her cupped hands, "Get that thing away from me!"

"So you don't eat meat?" the distorted voice said. "No meat at all?"

"Are you deaf? I said I was a vegan. Nothing's changed in the three seconds since I told you!"

"What about fish?" the voice asked.

"Oh, gee," Whisper said, slapping a palm against her forehead. "Is fish a plant? A lot's changed since I was in SEV-ENTH GRADE BIOLOGY!"

Then the speakers clicked off and the room was silent once more.

"Oh my god..." Whisper moaned. "Oooohhhhh myyyy gawwd! I can't breathe...you're literally keeping me from breathing!" She clapped a hand over her nose and mouth. She looked around the cell and grabbed a blanket off the cot, then stood up and walked as close to the table as she could bear.

"Oh god..." The smell of the ham was beginning to seep through her fingers. She could feel her stomach beginning to churn as she began to swing the blanket back and forth, releasing it just as it arced out. It landed on the sandwich, covering it, and she whooped in victory.

"Now get it out of here!" she shouted.

"No," the voice said.

"Why not?" Whisper whined.

"Because you're a rude person."

Whisper laughed. "I'm rude? You're the one who captured me and put me in this hellhole with a murder sandwich."

"Why are you calling it that?" the voice asked.

"Calling it what?" Whisper asked.

"A 'murder sandwich'. It's a ham sandwich."

"Why are you calling it ham?" Whisper shot back. "It didn't stop being a pig when you killed it. It's a pig sandwich. A pig impregnated against its will. Injected. Caged. Trapped. Slaughtered. Murdered!"

She had worked herself up into a foaming frenzy. She hadn't been this worked up since the Annul Animal Husbandry march.

The voice remained silent.

"Run out of ignorant questions?" she spat.

No answer.

"That's good!" she shouted. "I am a worthy woman. Just because that scares you doesn't mean you can question my choices, you backwoods, MAGA bastard."

A door screeched open on a track, then squawked shut.

The fat man who now stood in front of the cage wore a rubber pug mask.

"That's offensive," Whisper stated.

"Offensive how?"

"You don't see animals wearing human masks."

"Why would they...What..." The stranger was dumbstruck.

"Get this sandwich out of here," Whisper said. "I literally can't breathe with it in here."

Pug Head looked at her with his head cocked to the side.

"What are you waiting for?" Whisper shrieked.

Pug Head jumped, unlocked the door, and removed the ham sandwich.

"She says she can't breathe with it in there," Albie said, putting the plate on the control room table.

"What a bitch," Donald said.

"Well, what was I supposed to do?" Albie asked, yanking the pug mask off his head.

"Tell the spoiled brat to suck it up. We're not a Burger King. She can't have it her way this time."

"I don't think a Burger King would suit her any better," Albie said. He looked at the sandwich longingly; save for a few stray blanket threads stuck to it, it was still perfectly good.

"Don't even think about it," Donald said, leaning back in

his chair and passing a bag of apple chips to Albie. "Doctor's orders."

Albie sat at the monitors with a sigh and plunged his hand into the bag.

"Vegan," Donald said. "The brat's family is loaded and she decides to eat plants her whole life. So many people in the world don't have access to meat–"

"Or aren't allowed to eat it," Albie said miserably.

"–and she flat out refuses. Probably eats tofu...you two should talk recipes," Donald mocked.

"Tofu's expensive," Albie said. "And for something so bland..." He rubbed his finger over the call button for a moment and then pressed it.

"Do you eat tofu?" he asked into the microphone.

On the monitor, Whisper's head lolled back as she rolled her eyes.

"Yeaausss!" she groaned.

"How?" Albie asked.

"With my fucking mouth, you idiot."

"Wow," Donald said.

I know! Albie mouthed. Then he turned back to the intercom. "No, I mean how can you stand it? It's so bland."

"Um, I don't know," Whisper said, crossing her arms beneath her breasts. "How do you stand eating handfuls of flour? It's so bland!"

"Handfuls of—" Albie threw his hand in the air, giving up.

"Is ten mil enough?" Donald asked. "Really, I ask you. Is it enough to keep this nasty cow alive?"

"Maybe she's just lashing out," Albie said.

"I can understand 'lashing out'," Donald said. "She's chained up. She doesn't know where she is. I get that. But that's not why she's lashing out. She's lashing out because you tried to serve her a ham sandwich."

"A nice ham sandwich," Albie said, eyeing it once more.

"A very nice ham sandwich," Donald agreed. "From a damn fine cook. I don't care if you're the Queen of England, if I give you something to eat and you talk to me like that..."

"And isn't that how we got into this mess in the first place?" Albie asked. "Because you couldn't control your temper?"

"No!" Donald said, sitting up and sticking his finger in Albie's face. "No! We are in this mess because you had your father get me a job in his restaurant after I told you I wasn't good with people."

"You shoved a Monte Cristo down a woman's throat," Albie said.

"She said it was too dry!" Donald snapped. "Your sandwiches are freaking ambrosia compared to what that fat cow ate on a daily basis. She should have—"

"And I appreciate that," Albie said, meaning it. No one had ever stood up for him the way Donald did. It's what he loved about him. "But now we are trying it your way, alright? And you have to keep a cool head or else you might —" he paused, remembering their couples therapy, "—*we* might mess this up."

Albie took Donald's hand and they did their breathing exercises. When they had finished, Albie gave Donald a gentle kiss.

"Hey!" Whisper's voice shouted through the speakers. "Hey! I'm starving in here!"

"I hate her," Donald said, turning back to his computer. "I hate her, Albie, I really do."

"Should I make her something else to eat?" Albie asked.

"No," Donald said, "If she wants to eat, she will eat the sandwich. Her father will call to confirm the drop and then we'll get her out of here. She can compromise her morals for another few hours."

"Hey! Asshole!" Whisper's voice screeched.

Albie thumbed the button and spoke.

"I made you a perfectly good sandwich. Free range ham, homemade bread, homemade provolone, brown mustard, and a boatload of love. You can eat my sandwich or you can starve. Make your choice."

"That's more like it," Donald laughed.

"Right?" Albie said.

Whisper began to howl like a wounded animal. Albie looked back to the screen and cried out. The girl was bashing her head against the concrete wall.

"Jesus!" Albie screamed. He pressed the button. "Stop that right now!"

"No!" Whisper screamed. "Not until you bring me gluten-free avocado toast." She slammed her head against the wall again.

"Gluten-free?" Albie looked helplessly at Donald.

"That stupid, spoiled brat," Donald hissed.

Then the burner phone rang.

"Shit," Donald said. "Go stop her!"

"How do I—?"

Donald grabbed the sandwich and slapped it into Albie's hand. "Tell her to cut it out or you'll shove that sandwich down her throat." He put one of the voice distorters to his mouth and answered the phone as Albie ran out of the room.

"I believe I have made myself perfectly clear," Mr. Meadows said. "I'm not giving you a damn penny for her."

Donald needed to do his breathing exercises and he needed to do them now. He and his therapist had figured out that when his ears burned like they were doing now, he was close to losing his temper.

"And that," she had said, with her plump, happy face, "isn't good for anyone."

But he couldn't count to ten right now. Hell, he couldn't even count to two: Mr. Meadows would hang up on him and the whole plan would be ruined.

"I don't think you understand, Mr. Meadows—" he began.

"No," Meadows interrupted. "I don't think *you* understand, bucko. I sent her to college a Young Republican and she came back a bisexual vegan named Whisper. She cost me a Senate race. She put her mother into an early grave. The little witch will do anything just to spite you and I am glad to be rid of her."

There was a click on the other line.

"Hello? Hello?"

Donald threw the burner phone against the wall. His ears burned as he grabbed one of the monitors and threw it to the floor. He kicked it for good measure, breaking two of his toes. Screaming, he grabbed the sandwich plate and smashed it against the wall.

"I am NOT eating your disgusting sandwich. Bring it near me and I will throttle you with this chain!"

Donald looked at the other monitor.

Whisper had managed to cut a nice gash across her forehead. Her bared teeth stood out bright against her blood-stained face. Albie walked into the cage, his stupid pug mask looking up at one of the cameras. When he got near enough she kicked him in the crotch.

Albie dropped the sandwich.

Whisper lunged at him. She wrapped her chain around his throat and began to strangle him.

Donald heard blood pulsing in his ears.

"Ungrateful..." Donald hissed through gritted teeth. "Spoiled...spiteful...little..."

He roared in agony as he put weight on his broken toes, bent down, and swiped up a shard of broken plate and began to hop down the hall toward Albie.

When he entered the cage, Whisper screamed, released Albie, and backed away.

"There are two of you?" she shouted.

"Donald," Albie coughed. "I'm sorry, she—"

Donald pushed past Albie, scooped up the sandwich and stalked toward Whisper.

"Men!" Whisper shouted. "You just hate it when a woman is stronger than—"

"Shut. Up!" Donald shouted. "Shut up! Shut! Up!"

Whisper's mouth puckered and her eyes flashed with white hot rage.

"You have three choices, you spiteful little witch. Eat the sandwich. Starve. Slit your wrists. Your choice." Donald dropped the broken piece of plate onto the cot and the sandwich on the floor. The ham—now cold with congealed cheese on top—slid out from between the mustardy bread.

"Donald..." Albie said.

"Albie, shut up and get back to the control room now!"

"DONALD!" Albie screamed.

Donald turned, certain he would see the piece of ceramic plate heading toward his eye. Sure that all the pressure of the world would explode with his ruptured eyeball, he almost welcomed it.

Instead, he saw Whisper sit on the edge of the cot, put the blanket in her mouth, bit down, and put the shard of plate against her chained ankle.

"Oh," Donald said.

Then Whisper sawed into her flesh.

Albie began to scream, the pug mask still half over his head, clutching at his chest. Donald stepped onto his bad foot and fell to the floor, looking up at Whisper in sheer amazement. She looked right back at him, her eyes filled with tears, yet unflinching. Fillets of flesh folded over her foot, exposing the pale bone beneath.

She tried to saw through it, the sound of silverware on china filling the room, making Donald want to vomit.

"Donald...Donald," Albie said. The weakness in his voice shook Donald out of his shock. He looked around and saw that Albie was clutching at the side of his throat, eyes wide. Donald crawled to Albie and cradled him.

Whisper, still looking directly into Donald's eyes, slid off the cot and into the pool of her own blood, crawled toward the nearest set of bars, and slid her mangled foot between them.

"No..." Albie wheezed.

"No..." Donald whispered.

Whisper nodded.

A sickening crack.

An ear-splitting scream.

Whisper was free.

Albie's considerable weight fell on top of Donald, pinning him to the floor. Albie's wide eyes stared down at him, through the pug mask. He didn't make a sound.

"Albie?" Donald tried pushing him off, but all his energy had been sapped by what he had just witnessed. The image of the bone snapping like a twig played over and over again in his mind. "Albie, she's getting away. She's—"

At some point, Whisper had tied the blanket around her

leg, and was now crawling across the threshold of the cage.

"Albie, get up! She's—"

Panic gripped Donald's stomach.

"Please!" he cried out. "Please, call an ambulance. He's had a heart attack. He's—"

She turned to look back at him and, using her good leg, slammed the cage door shut.

The lock clicked.

"Enjoy your damn sandwich," Whisper said.

It was quite impressive, actually. Her father had been right; through sheer spite, she was holding back any cry of agony, any sign of weakness. She crawled away, leaving a trail of blood, her captors, and the murder sandwich behind her.

Donald rested his head on the cold, blood-drenched floor and stared at the deconstructed ham sandwich and wondered how long he could make it last.

Overdue Notice

Andrew Johnston

10/01/15 9:37 AM
From: Paradise Gardens Public Library Services
To: Richard Munroe
RE: Overdue Notice

Hello, sir. This is to inform you that you now have four items that are past their due date. These items will accrue 15 cents each in fines per day until returned. Additionally, if the items are not returned within 30 days, additional fines will be levied and we will take measures to retrieve the overdue materials.

Thank you for using our services, and we hope to see you soon.

10/03/15 10:02 AM
From: Paradise Gardens Public Library Services
To: Richard Munroe
RE: Follow-Up

Hello, sir. I am following up on a previous notification

for several items you have checked out, which are now three days overdue. I feel you should know that one of those items has had a request for over three weeks. This means that one of our other patrons is patiently waiting for you to return your materials. We hope that you can find the time in the next few days to drop by the library, return your materials and pay our fine, which is currently a mere $1.80.

Thank you.

10/07/15 12:40 PM
From: Paradise Gardens Public Library Services
To: Richard Munroe
RE: Notification

Good afternoon, sir. I don't wish to intrude on your time, but I felt you should know that you have several very popular items in your possession. I have requests for three of them, with one in particular acquiring an impressive waiting list.

At the library, we do realize that there are often very good reasons why a patron cannot return his or her items in a timely fashion. In the event of, for example, a sudden death in the family or a serious personal injury, it may not be practical to visit the library in person. If this is the case, please inform me and we will ease back on further notifications and find an alternative means of returning your items. If you do not have such an excuse, rest assured that we are more than capable of furnishing one for you.

Your current fine is $4.20, which I think you will agree is very reasonable given the services the library provides.

Thank you.

10/10/15 9:13 AM
From: Paradise Gardens Public Library Services
To: Richard Munroe
RE: Your Account

Good morning, sir. I take it from your recent response that you found the notice that our agents left in your living room. Normally, we would not resort to such assertive tactics after less than two weeks, but given the number of patrons waiting for the items in your possession, we felt it prudent to accelerate our timetable by a few days.

Before you go to the police, you should note that our agents did not damage, steal or even search anything in your home. There has been no harm and, as you will discover, no physical evidence was left. Note that we did not retrieve the overdue items at this point—returning those (and paying the $6.00 fine) is your job as a responsible adult.

Thank you, sir, and we hope we do not have to resort to further means to enforce our policies.

10/14/15 12:56 PM
From: Paradise Gardens Public Library Services
To: Richard Munroe
RE: An interesting story

Good afternoon, sir. I was catching up on the news this morning when I spotted a story that I thought might be most interesting to you. It concerned a community not unlike our own with a library quite similar to, if not as expansive as, this one. One of the patrons decided he could turn a profit by stealing from the library before he skipped town. He opened multiple new accounts under the names of relatives and co-workers and used them to check out hundreds of items that he intended to sell on the second-hand market. He was only found out when the police apprehended him on an unrelated charge.

Isn't that awful, sir? Such things happen when a library fails to take adequate action to secure its materials. Of course, the blame ultimately lies with the perpetrator. I think you'll agree that there's no ditch in hell hot enough for someone who would betray his own community for such petty gain.

Incidentally, I saw you coming out of the Weighty Shelf yesterday. You didn't have anything with you—I assumed you were selling some items, perhaps to pay down your fine (currently $8.40). I do love the Weighty Shelf, although the staff could be a bit more attentive. On a few occasions, I have found stolen library materials among their stock. Fortunately, they are always very gracious in returning the materials and helping us find the perpetrators.

Thank you, sir, and have a good day.

10/16/15 9:39 AM
From: Paradise Gardens Public Library Services
To: Richard Munroe
RE: Your Account

I find your continued intransigence troubling, sir. Why are you so unwilling to live up to your obligations? I realize that to a man like yourself, our passion must seem perplexing. You must understand that a library is not merely a place for storing and lending books. It is a cornerstone of the community. Even as the short-sighted pundits and politicians have predicted the death of these institutions, libraries such as ours have grown and thrived. That's because the community recognizes the merits of the library and what it stands for.

I look at these walls and I see something beautiful—I see the future. I see a world in which information and resources are freely accessible to everyone, where needless struggle is replaced with the spirit of cooperation. It's not just me; we all share this vision. But every utopia has a critical flaw. You see, sir, for our vision to work, people have to respect the community and the people who live there. Without that respect, the system crumbles under the weight of the explorers.

That's why I must continue to apply pressure, sir. There is now a waiting list for every item you possess, and I must recover them by any means. If you can't respect our rules, then we'll have to resort to more intensive means to enforce them.

Good day, sir.

10/19/15 10:12 AM
From: Paradise Gardens Public Library Services
To: Richard Munroe

RE: (no subject)

Good morning, sir. I understand that you've recently had an opportunity to become personally acquainted with our agents and their advanced enforcement methods. I have in front of me a copy of your police complaint. We have already spoken with the police and explained to them that we had no role in your unfortunate accident. I think you'll find that they are likely to believe our version—you would be surprised how many of our patrons sever the first joint of their own left index finger while performing routine home maintenance.

Your fine is now $11.40. Please try and return your materials as soon as possible.

10/22/15 2:01 PM
From: Paradise Gardens Public Library Services
To: Richard Munroe
RE: Question

Sir, your routine is most puzzling to me. Several times a week, you walk through the downtown area, passing within a block of the library. You could easily detour to the library with minimal disruption to your schedule. Then again, as of late you've adopted a very circuitous path that must add thirty minutes to your routine. I can only surmise that you are trying to avoid passing by the library, something which is disturbing to me.

Is it possible that you have lost the materials that we lent you? In my experience, it is not uncommon for someone who has misplaced an item—or perhaps lent it to a less than trustworthy friend—to avoid reporting it, out of shame or a hope that he or she can recover the item in due time. In most cases, this only leads to further complications. If you have lost your materials, I would recommend reporting it immediately and paying your dues—the cost of the materials plus outstanding overdue fines and a restock penalty. This will not be cheap, but I believe you'll find it less costly than the consequences should you continue to ignore your responsibility.

10/24/15 11:31 AM
From: Paradise Gardens Public Library Services
To: Richard Munroe
RE: Good Morning

Hello, sir. One of my colleagues has informed me that you recently took your vehicle to the auto shop for a tune-up. Are you planning a trip out of town, by any chance? Here at the Paradise Gardens Public Library, we are happy to offer materials to patrons who travel extensively—indeed, many of our collegian patrons extensively employ our music CD collection on road trips. However, we do frown on individuals with extensive fines (and may I remind you that yours now exceed $14.00) taking materials outside the city limits. I hope you understand.

\----------

10/26/15 3:18 PM
From: Paradise Gardens Public Library Services
To: Richard Munroe
RE: Something to consider

I've been reading a lot of history lately, sir. I wanted to figure out why powerful men fear educators so much. Did you know that the Qin Emperor tried to have every scholar of Confucianism killed? But it's not just the ancient age, sir. There were plenty of teachers lying in shallow graves in Katyn Forest after Stalin was finished, alongside soldiers and police. Even the wealthiest men of our own age seem obsessed with eliminating teachers and librarians, albeit by less savage means. They bleed us a dollar at a time with hopes of replacing us with their own loyal agents.

What is it about us that invokes such terror, sir? I think it's our creativity that they fear. In other times, the masses were ignorant due to lack of opportunity. Today, the cause is numbness brought about by a lifetime of overstimulation. I don't blame the entertainment, sir—it would be hypocritical given the media library I help to maintain—it is merely a fact of life. Most people lack either the opportunity or the motivation to truly contemplate the nature of things.

We, on the other hand, possess both the opportunity and the motivation to truly exercise our creativity. My mind is operating at full speed all day, weaving new worlds of possibility that may one day exist. One of those worlds involves you, sir. I would tell you about it, but if you continue to ignore our requests you shall soon find yourself living in it. Suffice it to say, sir, that losing part of a finger is far from the worst thing that can happen to a betrayer of his community.

10/29/15 4:03 PM
From: Paradise Gardens Public Library Services
To: Richard Munroe
RE: (no subject)

Our patience is not infinite, sir.

10/30/15 9:01 PM

From: Paradise Gardens Public Library Services

To: Richard Munroe

RE: Final Notice

I am sorely disappointed, sir. I truly believed that we could come to a civil agreement and end this amicably. However, you have proven time and time again that you are not willing to live up to your obligations, so now we have to resort to more extreme methods.

Have you ever heard of the phenomenon of the disappearances? Paradise Gardens has a disproportionately large number of missing persons, a rate of disappearances far beyond what one would expect based on our demographics. This has been true since the early days of the township. There's an old myth that the statue in Mansion Park bears a hex, that anyone who falls asleep at its base is destined to be dragged off to the land of lost souls. An interesting superstition, but one that does little to explain why so many people simply depart without warning.

But not every disappearance is a mystery, sir. The most recent missing person was a woman named Layla. She was a frequent visitor to the library, so I knew her far too well. A most unpleasant woman, rude and irresponsible. She ran up over a hundred dollars in fines over the years, of which she paid back only the smallest fraction despite having the means to settle the balance at once. She vanished a few months back, and the police have long since called off their search. In a place with so many disappearances, one more is scarcely acknowledged, even by the authorities.

Do you want to know the truth, sir? The police called off their search because we told them to call off their search. And why should they waste their time? She's not truly missing, sir. I know where Layla is. I also know where you are, sir, although I imagine that you are more mobile than she is.

10/31/15 1:41 AM
From: Paradise Gardens Public Library Services
To: Richard Munroe
RE: (no subject)

If you haven't yet, sir, I suggest you start running.

11/02/15 9:55 AM
From: Paradise Gardens Public Library Services
To: Paula Anderson
RE: Item Request Notice

Good morning, ma'am. I'm pleased to inform you that

the item you requested is now available. You can pick it up on the hold shelf at your convenience. We appreciate your patience. Remember: Even though you had to wait, you are still responsible for returning this item in a timely fashion and paying the price should you fail to do so.

Thank you for using our services, and we hope to see you soon.

Bad Dates and Dragons

Alyssa Eckles

As far as bad dates went, this was one of the worst. Maria had a friend pulled up on her phone just beneath the edge of the high-top table, a 'save me' text ready to send, when her date mentioned his brand-new dragon.

"What?" Maria asked, thumb hovering over the pulsing green Send button. "You have a *dragon?*"

"Well, actually," her date, Devon, said, "It's a wyvern, but I've found most people have no idea what that is. A wyvern —"

"I know what a wyvern is," Maria said. *Did this guy just 'well, actually' me?*

With a move he obviously assumed was very smooth, Devon leaned over the small, sticky tabletop, catching her free hand with one of his own. His thumb skimmed across the back of her hand, his eyes flicking up to hers with a practiced smolder that left Maria feeling in need of a nice, hot bleach bath.

"What say we—" He paused. *Uuuuuugh. Seriously.* "—get out of here and you can see it for yourself."

And that was how, at 10:12 p.m. on a Thursday, Maria stood in a condo driveway two neighborhoods away, watching as the worst date of her life fumbled to open his garage door to show off his dragon.

She had had sort-of high hopes, of course. They'd matched online, an 87% compatibility. He'd had photos of himself rock climbing, beside a fire with an assortment of neutral white men, holding a dog that was obviously not his, staring into a picturesque sunset. His favorite food was tacos. He enjoyed sports. He liked to laugh—"LOL", to quote his profile. He was perfectly fine, someone who wouldn't murder her at his first chance with a slightly sharp butter knife, but he also wasn't the one she'd bring home to Mom and Dad. Still, a date was a date, and Maria needed a drink.

So when Thursday evening found her across the table from a man who was slightly older, shorter, and less Instagram-able than his profile had suggested, Maria began to regret her decision.

Devon was in finance. Or, that's all he'd say about his work, other than it was aggressive and demanding and *so* rewarding. He asked her what her favorite book was, but then began to talk about how Kerouac was truly a visionary who changed his life. He chatted with the waiter for seven minutes on the best wine, where in Napa Valley it was made, how uninformed some people were about sommelier culture, and ended up with a cheap merlot. He asked why her last relationship failed, and speculated aloud on how humans are so complex sometimes, you know? He was, in what would be agreed upon by every woman in the history of everything, the literal worst.

Yet here she was, fidgeting from foot to foot as Devon finally managed to unlock and raise his garage door. Inside was rather pristine: a woodworking bench that obviously belonged to the previous tenant, some garbage cans, and a few classic rock posters that looked too glossy to be originals. A hulking wire cage dominated the back of the garage, and something chittered from among the shredded newspaper lining it.

"Come on in," Devon said, ushering Maria forward, his hand pressed against the small of her back. *This guy is more handsy than a second-rate magician*, she thought, and hurried out of range of his touch. Metal rumbled, and Maria watched hesitantly as Devon pulled the door closed after them.

"To keep the heat in," he said. "Wyverns are cold-blooded, you see, so they need other warm—"

"I know," Maria said, forcing a smile. This was a mistake. No wyvern was worth listening to this guy talk down to her another minute more.

A sharp rustle of paper made her change her opinion, and she hurried over to the cage with childlike glee.

The enclosure was nearly eight square feet, reaching almost to the ceiling, where a nylon mesh topped the cage in a grid of silvery webbing. The bars were surprisingly flimsy, considering what it potentially contained, and seemed better suited for a medium-sized dog than a dragon. Weeks-worth of newspaper pillowed on the concrete floor, shredded loops rustling as something moved beneath them. On either end of the cage, two tall carpet-wrapped cat trees towered, deep rents down their lengths in regular, vicious lines. The catnip mice dangling from them, though, were unscathed.

"Let's see if he's hungry," Devon said behind her, and Maria managed to avoid flinching at his sudden nearness. He stooped beside the woodworking bench and opened a short, squat refrigerator. Cans of cheap beer lined the door, and stacks of paper-wrapped packets filled the shelves. He selected one, tearing away the casing to reveal purpled meat. The smell of iron tinged the air, and Maria jumped as a shape lunged from beneath the newspaper litter in the cage.

It was *beautiful*. Red-black skin, pebbled and shiny, covered its length from nose to tail. Gold eyes widened above a broad-nosed snout, staring as Devon approached with its meal. It clung to the side of a cat tree with two strong feet, three-inch claws biting deep. Arched over its back, half-unfurled, was a pair of membranous dark wings.

"I've never seen one up close before," Maria breathed, standing as near to the wire bars as she dared.

Devon stuck his hand quickly through a gap in the cage, tossing the dripping meat in the air. The wyvern's neck stretched out, long jaws unhinging, and the steak disappeared forever in a fury of teeth. Maria, smartly, jumped back from the cage.

"His name is Draconus," Devon said. "That means, 'dragon king'."

Of course it did.

"Not 'dragon queen'?" Maria asked.

Devon looked at her, the corners of his smarmy smirk pulling downward. Maria pointed at the wyvern, still watching them, unblinking, as a cherry-colored tongue flicked hungrily.

"It's a female," she said.

Devon's frown intensified.

"Males have pronounced dewlaps, used in mating performances. Yours has a small dewlap, same color as her underbelly. I don't think she's even sexually mature yet, given her size."

"Oh," Devon said. Maria could tell he wasn't quite following, though he had perked up at the mention of "sexually." He leaned close, sliding his arm around her waist. Maria squirmed at his touch.

"Where did you say you got her?" she asked.

"I've got this friend. His buddy imports exotic animals, the more dangerous the better. Tigers, chimeras, sharks. Got this one brought in special at my request. Cost me a couple grand. Five thousand, actually. They're super illegal, you know," Devon said, confident again. His words practically oozed from his mouth. His hand, too, felt slimy as it slid down her rear.

"I know," Maria said. "That's why I'm surprised you told me you had one."

"Oh?" Devon slithered even closer.

"Because of my job."

"Yeah?" He pressed against her. *That had better be an*

unripe banana stuffed down his pants…

"At the Department of Exotic and Magical Animal Protection."

"What?" Finally, it was Devon who recoiled.

"Yes," Maria said. "I told you that. When we were ordering drinks."

"You didn't say that," he protested.

"Yes, I did. It was on my profile, too," Maria said. "And that I studied magibiology at university. Didn't you notice?"

"But you don't really… I mean, you're like an assistant or something."

"No, I'm a coordinator for animal seizure and reintroduction." Maria frowned. "You seriously didn't listen to anything I said?"

"Um…"

Devon had finally released his grip on her, backing away. His eyes flitted to the garage door, to the cage, and back to Maria. He was starting to look a little green.

Maria heaved a sigh, crossing her arms. She needed to delete that dating app when she got home.

"Look. I'll get you some paperwork, maybe see if there's a loophole where you could keep her," she said. "You'd have to increase her habitat, though, and stop feeding her red meat. Wyverns are piscivores. Fresh fish, preferably saltwater, though you can probably get by with a sodium supplement if you can't get that. And you might have to classify your house as a conservation center."

"Wait, you're going to tell on me?" Devon said. His

cheeks flushed from green to a boiling puce in an instant.

"This isn't kindergarten," Maria snapped. "This is my job, and you're housing a violent reptile in a residential neighborhood. It's a matter of time before your neighbors' kids become snacks for this thing!"

"You can't!"

This idiot... Maria wondered how soon a ride could get here if she called for one now. With a sigh, she pulled out her phone, opening the cab app when a blunt slap sent the screen flying from her grasp.

"Hey!"

"If you tell, I'll... I'll..." Devon was practically spitting in his panic, fists clenched as he attempted to loom over her. Which was something. Maria had worn heels, after all, assuming his profile's stated height had been truthful.

"I'm leaving," Maria said.

She turned toward the garage door and her flung phone —now with a broken screen, *great*—when Devon wrapped a hand around her upper arm and yanked her back. She staggered, her shoulders striking the cage with a frightening rattle and clank. The whole enclosure shuddered, and the wyvern hissed inside. Maria pushed herself off the metal grid but Devon shoved her back again. The bars rattled, the joints creaked, and before she knew it, Maria was sprawled on the collapsed remains of the wyvern's cage.

Some people claim their lives flash before their eyes at their imminent death. For Maria, the only things flashing before her eyes were the dating profiles she could have chosen over Devon's. She could be eating tapas with that pharmacy student, or visiting a museum with that cashier, or even having awkward chit-chat with that guy who just sent her the message 'U up?' at 3 a.m. every Tuesday. Instead, she was lying on her back, on a dangerous animal's crumpled enclosure, with a frightening man standing over her. Yes, even 'U up?' would be better than this.

"Look what you did!" Devon howled. "That cost three hundred dollars! You'll pay for that, you dumb b—"

All Maria saw next was a blur of inky darkness, a high-pitched shriek, a spray of red arcing across the bare-bulb lights. Pushing herself up to her elbows, she watched as an arm, probably the one that had minutes ago been happily groping her backside, shuddered down the gullet of Draconus. Jaws unhinged and spread wide, the wyvern tore another meal from what had once been Devon—a nice leg this time. It was like a child destroying a ragdoll, easily done with the right rips and tears, but with much more viscera, blood, and delighted squeals. Or at least slightly more.

Maria knew she should be horrified. A man was being eaten alive, after all. But somehow, she couldn't bring herself to look away from the feeding frenzy, let alone care.

Probably due to the violent threats. Or was it the mansplaining? Nah, mostly it was the violent threats.

With much undulating of throat and a nauseating gagging sound, Devon's khaki boat shoe vanished into the distended belly of the wyvern. Draconus rustled her wings, allowing their true width to be glimpsed for an instant as her tips brushed the ceiling, before pulling them in tightly to her back. She crawled on top of what remained of her meal, kneading her claws like a common housecat, before comfortably coiling her tail around her sated bulk.

"I guess you don't mind red meat, after all," Maria said.

Draconus didn't respond, though she did turn her sleepy eyes toward Maria. The wyvern looked positively pleased.

Maria crawled to her knees, avoiding the broken bars and metal joints of the cage as best she could. With her eyes on the wyvern, she stretched out for her phone, fingers fumbling until the comforting square was in range to be dragged back to her. Scrolling through her contacts, Maria dialed her boss.

"Prishi? It's Espinosa," she said. "…Yeah, the date didn't go so great. I know, I know. Could you pick me up? And… what's the largest dog carrier we have at the station? Yeah, we're going to need that. Oh, and the police, if you don't mind. They're going to want to see this."

From her nest atop Devon's bloodied torso, Draconus yawned. Nestling her snout between her claws, she closed her eyes and had a much-deserved nap.

The Haunting of Peruvius Corcorant

George Nikolopoulos

Peruvius Corcorant watched the yurei as it hovered a couple of feet above the living room floor, head hung low, arms outstretched and hands dangling from the wrists, the tiny ghost's morose expression mirroring his own. He just wanted to watch the ball game, but it proved impossible as the ghost floated to and fro in front of the TV set, as if its sole purpose in the afterlife was to prevent him from any enjoyment.

He supposed that it had all been Lyra's fault. Peruvius had decided to throw a Halloween party for his office colleagues, mostly to impress her—well, he wanted to impress his boss too, of course, but he liked to think he did it for her. When he told her that he was thinking of getting a super-hero for the party, however, she jeered at him.

"A superhero, Peru? Are you serious? Why don't you get an accountant instead, he'd be much more entertaining. I mean, superheroes are so last year, so boring. But don't you worry; your little Lyra is here to help and I know exactly what you should get for our party: a ghost. Ghosts are so reckless and wild, they're loads of fun."

Peruvius was neither reckless nor wild, and his idea of fun was taking out his collection of late Victorian buttons to give them a good brushing—but if he threw a party to entice Lyra it wouldn't do at all to ignore her wish. That was why, the next evening, his unwilling feet carried him to Ghunnar Ghulam's Ghastly Ghostarium.

The venerable spectral emporium was housed in a ramshackle building in the heart of the Old Town, next to a tandoori joint. Ghunnar himself was a tiny guy with a huge mouth and small, beady eyes that kept darting from one place to the next and never seemed to stand still.

Aromas of cumin and cinnamon lay thick in the air. Peruvius took a deep breath and choked. "Um, I'd like to buy a... you know, a ghost," he said with a pitiful display of eloquence while trying to regain his composure.

Ghunnar laughed. "A ghost, *naturally*. You've come to the right place; we do sell ghosts here. Only the finest, sir, only the finest! What kind of ghost would you like? A spook, a poltergeist, a wraith, a bogeyman?"

"Um, a... you know, something to haunt a house, for a party," said Peruvius, feeling increasingly uncomfortable. "Something... fun?" he ventured.

"An excellent choice," said Ghunnar. "What about a pirate? May I suggest Blackbeard?" As he spoke, a burly pirate rose through the floor to hover in front of Peruvius. He looked quite menacing with his huge black beard, eye patch, hook and peg leg. Even the parrot perched on his shoulder looked frightening.

Peruvius gulped. "No, not really," he said in a small voice.

"You sure, mate? Because damn me to hell if this here pirate's not t' life o' t' party, Blackbeard is, yar-har-har, aye-aye me laddie." It took Peruvius a moment to realize Ghunnar was now impersonating a pirate and failing miserably. He must have realized it himself because, thankfully, he reverted to his ordinary irritating salesman's voice. "And if you don't fancy black, he comes in an astounding variety of colors," he said. "We've got Bluebeard, Redbeard—" a number of pirates with variously colored beards appeared through the floor as he spoke. "How about Pinkbeard over there?"

Peruvius was inordinately terrified, and for some strange reason Pinkbeard seemed the scariest of the lot. "Um, I'd rather not," he said. "Please?"

Ghunnar waved his hand and the pirates disappeared. "What do you think of Red Baron?" he said. "Everyone loves Red Baron." A ghostly biplane with a painted black cross swooped down before Peruvius, a grinning red skull behind the wheel.

"No!" he almost shouted.

"The Flying Dutchman, then. What an original idea!" A spectral ship sailed through the wall, crewed by a skeleton army. "Yo-ho-ho and a bottle o' rum!"

"No more pirates!"

"Well, you're a lucky fella, because this week we have a big discount on Hamlet's father. But know, thou noble youth, the serpent that did sting thy Father's life, blah blah blah and all of that."

"Um... anything else?"

Ghunnar elbowed him and winked. "I know exactly what you have in mind," he said. "I have a great line of female ghosts, real foxy ladies. You know, ghosts are not nearly as incorporeal as people think."

Peruvius blushed. "I don't think my girlfriend would appreciate it."

At that precise moment, a small, white-robed figure with long, black, disheveled hair, wandered into the room, seemingly of its own volition. Hands dangling from outstretched wrists, it floated a few feet above the floor—which was fitting, as it didn't seem to have any legs or feet.

"Um, what is that?"

"A Japanese ghost, a yurei," said Ghunnar with an exasperated expression. A moment later, his eyes narrowed and he looked at Peruvius calculatingly. "Tell me, my good sir, what do you make of it?"

"Well," Peruvius was at a loss for words. "It seems rather harmless."

Ghunnar approached and took him by the arm. "What is your opinion of Japanese popular culture?"

"I love sushi," Peruvius said uncertainly.

Ghunnar smiled widely, revealing an impossible number of teeth inside his imposing mouth. "Then you'll love a yurei," he said.

The party was considerably less of a roaring success than Peruvius had expected.

As the little ghost wandered into the room, a heavy veil of heartbreaking gloom seemed to follow it. Almost at once people began to leave the party, at first offering some lame excuses and by the end practically running away. There was a commotion at the front door, and a fistfight nearly broke out.

Lyra left the party sobbing, and never spoke to Peruvius again.

His boss's wife was so depressed she suffered a nervous breakdown. A couple of days later, Peruvius was fired.

"Your advertisement said that if I was not satisfied I would get my money back. I'm categorically not satisfied."

Ghunnar shook his head so quickly it made Peruvius dizzy. "Not for this line of products," he said. "Unfortunately, there's no policy of refund or cancellation concerning the yurei." He showed Peruvius a footnote in extremely minuscule letters.

"But you *told* me I could return it in ten days if I changed my mind," insisted Peruvius.

"You can return it without compensation," said Ghunnar very slowly. "If you bring it back in its original packaging."

For a long time they stared silently at each other, the only sound to be heard the raucous laughter of some drunken pirates beneath the floor.

Peruvius was first to break. "I don't have the original

packaging," he said. "Will you just take it back for free?" He was on the verge of tears. "Please?"

Ghunnar shrugged. "I could do that, just for you," he said. "As a personal favor."

Peruvius' spirits lifted. "Will you come and collect it?"

Ghunnar stared at him, implacable. "I'm afraid you'll have to bring it to us."

"But I can't," said Peruvius. "I can't. When I see the yurei, my resolution melts away like dew before the morning sun. There's no way I can pick it up and return it to you."

Ghunnar smiled ruefully. "I know," he said. "The yurei feeds on desperation. It gets high on hopelessness. It will never leave you of its own accord." His face softened, making him look almost sympathetic. "Here's a free piece of advice," he said. "Seek professional help."

Peruvius opened the door in response to the insistent ringing of the doorbell.

She stood on the doorstep, six feet tall and full of muscles. She wore a wide-brimmed hat, a leather vest and breeches. Just one look at her and he was lost forever.

"Hello, Miss..."

"Ms. Amelia Applebottom, ghost hunter extraordinaire. You have requested my services." Her voice was candyfloss on a summer night, her eyes icicles on a winter morning. Peruvius was madly, desperately, hopelessly in love.

It's no use, he thought. *She'll take a look at the yurei and leave in tatters like all the other ghost exterminators who came before. I'll still be stuck with the ghost and I will never see her again.*

The yurei picked that moment to approach, its mournful expression sucking all mirth out of the universe.

Ms. Amelia seemed transfixed. "Oh dear," she said. "This is so very sad."

Peruvius' heart sank. He braced himself, waiting for her to turn tail and run.

The yurei stopped moving. It raised its head and stared at Ms. Amelia. She stared straight back. Peruvius experienced a rather peculiar feeling, as if a very heavy and gloomy veil was suddenly lifted.

"This dear child..." Amelia turned and looked at him. "Is she yours?"

"Um, she... Who?"

"I have to be a mother. I just realized I put it off for so long, it's really sad." She stared at Peruvius with an unfathomable expression. "Will you make me a mother?"

"Honey, I'm home!"

As she entered the apartment, Peruvius came rushing to give Amelia a kiss before kneeling to help her remove her boots.

"Where's Clementine?" she said.

The yurei floated through the wall, hands aimlessly dangling from its wrists. It wore a school uniform and its hair was done in pigtails.

Amelia looked at it with pride. "How was her first day at

school?" she asked.

Peruvius shrugged. "Great," he said. "She didn't cry at all." He was silent for a while. "All the other kids did. The teachers too. The principal begged us on his knees to never come back. He said he will post us a school graduation certificate. Or even a university degree."

Amelia smiled. "First day of school is always like that," she said. "In time, they'll all get used to it."

It Came from Mail Order

Eric J. Guignard

Jerry never imagined that a wrinkled old *Spider-Man* comic book could lead to death, mayhem, and, perhaps, worse. But if he were to look back at events, that was where it all began… the day he flipped that comic over and saw on its back cover the wildest of advertisements: a grainy, cartoonish ad that was all bubbles and smiling kids and promises of *Fun! Fun! Fun!*

An ad for Sea Monkeys.

It was 1972, and Jerry had never heard of such a thing. But there it was in print, like God's own truth, with a heart-stopping illustration showing families of pink-skinned mer-people just hangin' groovy in front of their underwater castle. They sure didn't look like 'monkeys' but, then again, he'd never contemplated what an aquatic primate *should* look like.

What were these sweet wonders of the ocean?!

The eighth-grader down the hall had traded the comic to him for some old photos Jerry found tucked in his mom's top dresser drawer of her looking all weird, nude in a field of wheat or something. But then, as much as Jerry loved *Spider-Man*, the web slinger was as forgotten as Tuesday's homework once he saw the Sea Monkeys.

The ad claimed: *Instant Pets—so eager to please they can even be trained!* And, when it seemed the deal couldn't get any finer, it even added: *Customers must be 100% satisfied with the Sea Monkeys or their money will be refunded!* For the cost of only one dollar (plus thirty cents S&H), he'd receive the Monkeys, their food, *and* the company's guarantee. Jerry couldn't believe the bargain; a spaz hamster cost two dollars and couldn't be trained to do anything.

He returned to his mom's top dresser drawer and rummaged around until he came out with a sticky dollar bill and three dimes. Carefully, he clipped out the order form and filled out his name and address in neat block letters, requesting the purchase be mailed posthaste to their apartment in San Francisco.

Jerry's brother, Luke, was four years older and too cool to be impressed by much, unless it was rock-and-roll, dope, or long-haired chicks protesting the War. But when Jerry told him about the Monkeys, Luke's fingers ran a riff of air guitar.

"That's Cool City!"

A long month passed until the Sea Monkeys finally arrived. It was a Saturday morning and one of the few times their mom was home between her three jobs.

When the postman made his delivery, Jerry was so excited he felt like he could run up the ceiling. "It's here, it's here!"

The box was labeled all over with big, bold words: *Caution, Live Organisms Within.* Holding it, Jerry's hands felt like they were filled with electricity. Luke joined him as Jerry tore open the packaging. But rather than any miniature monkeys, inside were three flat envelopes, each labeled with its contents: *Water Purifier*, *Food*, and *Sea Monkey Eggs*.

The electricity in Jerry's hands fizzled.

Luke made a stink-face. "What the...?"

They looked at each other, wondering how tiny envelopes of powder could turn into frolicking merpeople.

Alongside the envelopes lay a pamphlet explaining the official method to raise and train Sea Monkeys. There was also a certificate of ownership, reciting the company's guarantee of satisfaction or money back.

Jerry read the claims—just like in the original advertisement—and the excitement began to return. "Look, they promise our satisfaction. It must be for real!"

Their mom, Sharon, looked over their shoulders. "Oh, boys, I'm so pleased you have a new pet."

Though she smiled, Jerry noticed that she also cringed slightly, and he knew she remembered their last pet, a spotted hamster she'd brought home on Christmas. The brothers were wild with delight when they first saw little Fuzzy Jive Head, but then it died several weeks later. The tearful devastation he and Luke expressed at their pet's loss had not been truly *genuine* however...

What their mom didn't know was that he and Luke had just gotten bored with lil' Fuzzy. They forgot to feed it, and Luke had blown bong smoke at it with his friends one afternoon until the hamster fell over and never got back up.

"I hope you have fun with your Sea Monkeys," she said. "I've got to get ready for work."

Luke read the training instructions aloud, and Jerry cleaned out Fuzzy's old home, a five-gallon glass aquarium collecting cobwebs in the back of a cupboard.

"I'm going to teach the Sea Monkeys to jump through a hoop," Jerry vowed.

"I'm going to teach the Sea Monkeys to play air guitar," Luke pledged.

A pounding at the front door startled them both.

"Open up, it's Odie." The voice was gruff, tinged with cigarette ash and crust. It was the voice of a man wielding a bit of power and whose greatest pleasure was to squeeze every drop of leverage he could from that advantage. The voice was cold smiles and greasy hair... The voice was the landlord. "Rent's due."

Sharon's head popped out of the bedroom, angst caked over mascara and rouge. She motioned at the boys to be silent, but it was too late.

"I heard you in there. Don't play games with me!" Odie said, louder.

Sharon bit her lip and went to the door, wearing only a faded bathrobe.

"Hi, Odie, is it that time already?" Her voice rose a notch as she slipped out into the hallway, closing the door behind her.

Luke and Jerry stayed at the table, hearing only garbled bits of conversation.

"I'm a little short..." her voice.

"...last time..." his voice.

"Please..."

"...maybe work something out...*heh heh...*"

Sharon returned inside and slunk into her bedroom. The boys fell silent, the morning's elation flushed away by the crapper of reality.

Ten minutes later, their mom emerged in a striped waitress uniform. When she spoke, her voice was flat, and she didn't look at either of the boys. "I'll be home late after work. If you need anything, I'll be at... Odie's."

After she left, Luke muttered, "He'll get his one of these days."

Jerry didn't understand what his brother meant, but it sounded righteous.

They put their minds back to birthing Sea Monkeys like great gods breathing life into the mud of man, or some crap like that. Jerry filled the small aquarium with water, and Luke added the envelope of purifier. Together they opened up the tiny envelope titled, *Instant Live Eggs*, and poured the contents into the water. It looked like just a pile of yellow dust, like the kind you'd find under an unswept bed. Slowly, the minuscule eggs fell apart in the water and sank to the bottom of the aquarium.

The boys nodded to each other and watched, envisioning magical Sea Monkey shenanigans.

Nothing happened.

Jerry looked at the clock, then back to the instructions. "I guess it could take a few days to grow."

Luke rolled his eyes. There was nothing to do but wait.

Weeks later, the Monkeys were lamer than penny loafers at the school sock hop. The so-called 'Wonders of the Ocean' turned out to be nothing more than microscopic brine shrimp, looking like curly pubic hairs dangling in green-tinted water.

The Sea Monkeys didn't dance, didn't smile, didn't possess humanoid limbs or perform zany antics. Jerry couldn't imagine how they were considered *eager* to be taught *anything*. The Monkeys just floated, and their greatest achievement was occasionally drifting from one side of the aquarium to the other.

"This is totally square," Luke decried.

Jerry didn't say anything. He was too upset with the Monkeys to even vocalize his disappointment.

Their mom was away at work again that day. Rain poured outside. Luke picked at model airplane parts, gluing together random pieces from different kits with plastic cement. The aquarium of Sea Monkeys sat on the table while a Jimi Hendrix record played in the background. Jerry reread the Monkeys' instruction pamphlet and company guarantee for the hundredth time, trying to figure out what they'd done wrong in raising the bitty tots.

There was a lull in the music, and Luke filled it. "Hey, little brother, want to drop a tab?"

Jerry shrugged. "A tab of what?"

"Acid, man. LSD. Everyone's doing it."

"Doesn't acid burn you?"

"No, turd, it's not battery acid, it's a mind-enhancer. I took one already. Everything's *faaar-out*." Luke showed him a clear baggie containing small squares of blotter paper. "You just put one on your tongue and suck on it until it dissolves."

"Gross, I don't want to suck on paper."

Luke snickered. "You're so out of it. You'll never get laid, you know that?"

Jerry made a sour lemon-face and tossed the Monkeys' instruction pamphlet at him. Time ticked by. He muttered and sighed. Chewed a nail. Hummed a *Deep Purple* tune. Cupped his head in his hands and stared off into the ceiling, counting water stains. After a couple dozen of those, he sighed again and started picking at Luke's models. Pieces of airplanes, boats, and tanks overflowed a ratty shoebox and scattered across the table like the debris from some brutal massacre of toys.

Luke had gone silent, staring transfixed at the Sea Monkeys. "I'm trippin' balls, little brother."

"That sounds bad. You want to finish making this P-51?"

"Naw, but I know who does." Luke fingered the aquarium. "Those Sea Monkeys are bored in there! That's why they're just floating around—they're like us, with nothing much to do."

Luke took a tube of modeling cement and squeezed it out into the aquarium.

"What are you doing?" Jerry shouted. He tried to stop his

older brother, but Luke was stronger.

The glue floated on the water's surface like an oil slick. Monkeys that drifted into it were suddenly stuck and squirmed to escape. Luke took the fuselage of a plastic toy helicopter and dropped it in the water. The helicopter broke through the cement surface and sank, carrying glued Sea Monkeys to the bottom of the aquarium.

"Yeah, man, see?" Luke said. He added plastic tank treads, airplane cockpits, wheels, rotors, and another entire tube of glue. The shrimp flailed, spasming. "Now they're moving. With all those parts to choose from, maybe they'll build a Sea Monkey car."

Jerry stopped trying to fight Luke. Although part of him was horrified, another larger part realized it didn't really bother him at all watching their mail-order pets get tortured. Truth was, it was kind of satisfying seeing those phony Monkeys finally do something, even if it was struggling for life.

"They *are* pretty active now," he admitted.

"I told you they were bored. I bet their Sea Monkey car will be awesome!"

Jerry doubted that, but he shrugged his shoulders and went with it. "Think if we put wings in there, they'll make something that flies?"

"Yeah!" Luke picked out a pair of airplane wings and, adding more cement, dropped the wings into the aquarium.

After five minutes, a jumble of model parts lay at the bottom, and the water began to congeal from the glue. The Sea

Monkeys turned sluggish, and many sank.

Luke got angry. "What gives, man? We shared our toys and they're still not doing anything?"

"Stupid Sea Monkeys," Jerry agreed.

"What will it take to make them fun?" Luke's eyes drifted to the baggie of blotter paper on the table. "Maybe…"

He dropped an acid tab in the aquarium.

It dissolved quickly, and the cement-laden water flashed in the radiance of a thousand rainbows. Streaks of purple light twisted around red tracers, refracting over emerald veins. Turquoise and ice-white spots flared and burst in sparkle explosions like raining fireworks. The Sea Monkeys animated and began swimming in long, swooping arcs. Those glued to the model pieces moved as one, dragging the plastic parts behind them. Other Monkeys circled each other in a double-helix spiral, while electric-blue flashes flickered in their eyes, and the comic book smiles and crowns and antics seemed at last to be realized.

The brothers almost fell over. Jerry didn't know whether to laugh or run away, so he did both, and then returned to look closer. More bright fireworks erupted within, and the aquarium rocked gently back and forth as if to the tune of a magical song. Some Monkeys danced a conga line while others performed somersaults. Monkeys began to merge with one another. Where four shrimp squirmed only moments earlier, one larger shrimp appeared, the size of a mealworm.

It ended after the quickest ten minutes of Jerry's life. The colors of the water faded, and half-dead Monkeys floated listlessly to the surface.

"*Ho-lee* Moses," Luke whispered.

"Do it again," Jerry whispered even quieter.

Luke nodded reverently and dropped in another tab. The aquarium reanimated.

The Monkey frenzy grew, and they swung in dance like a concert troupe. More Monkeys merged together, and even those that had already done so merged again, so the conjoined bodies grew thick and sinewy. The aquarium shook with carousel delight.

Luke and Jerry shrieked with laughter.

The afternoon passed, and their mom came home. The brothers hid the Sea Monkeys in their shared bedroom until the following afternoon when she was again gone. Then they pulled out the aquarium, and Luke dropped in another tab. Monkey shenanigans resumed, and the boys were joyous.

They lost track of how many times they doped the aquarium over the following months. Neither brother ever provided food for the Monkeys; they just dropped in LSD or random pills or cigarette butts from Luke's friends. Rancid algae as toxic as nuclear sewage grew on the glass, but even that was beautiful when the acid-radiance began. The fluorescent green algae glimmered and flashed like strange Christmas light displays.

And in this environment—somehow—the Sea Monkeys thrived. They sustained themselves on the blooming algae, and their colony grew. Monkey eggs appeared in the filth and hatched into baby Sea Monkey mutants. The things that grew in the aquarium were nothing like the smiling merpeople Jerry first saw in the back of his *Spider-Man* comic. Instead, they were fleshy and tubular, like lengths of soft, pink noodles. Occasional groans rose from the mire and, more than once, Jerry thought he saw teeth materialize and snap shut against the glass.

Luke giggled and dropped in another acid tab. "It's feeding time."

The brothers watched as the Monkey-spectacle lit up once again. The water swirled in rainbow radiance, and the aquarium rocked back and forth like a record that spins warped on one side. Many of the Monkeys had melded together, transforming into slithering creatures, each with a hundred heads and tails. They still danced, but slower now. Fat, throbbing forms like red-veined slugs wrapped around themselves, forming trippy, ringed shapes.

Those shapes began to look very angry.

Suddenly, the rocking of the aquarium grew, starting to tumble back and forth like a wild, bucking horse trying to break its tether.

"Watch out!" Luke yelled, moments before it exploded in a kaleidoscope of dancing, singing colors. Both boys fell backward.

From the aquarium's fragments, a Sea Monkey-monster stood, pulsating, shards of glass embedded in its body like the razor quills of some demon porcupine.

Jerry gasped. "It's free..."

The creature turned to face the brothers, and they saw it as a gelatinous blob, maintaining the square shape of the five-gallon aquarium it'd grown in, like a quivering Jell-O removed from its mold.

The thing had a core of sloshing algae-filled water at its center, contained by the greasy, sticky jelly that composed its membrane skin. Mounds of misshapen plastic model parts were covered in squirming Sea Monkeys, and the Monkeys moved as one, splitting apart their own jelly mass, and casting out the shape of feet made from toy airplane wheels. Millions of Sea Monkey eyes blinked once across its body in rapid succession. The assemblage of its head was capped by the clear cockpit window of the model P-51.

It took a step toward them, then stopped, testing the limits of its movements. Even standing still, the body was never motionless—each frenzied little Monkey struggled in the greater form, causing the appearance of a television after the channel goes off-air, a wavering fuzzy static.

Luke moved to defend himself, grabbing a frayed baseball, then wavered between holding it out like some talisman of protection or pulling his arm back to throw it. He decided, and fired it hard at the creature. The ball shot through the air and sank into the thing's chest, like plopping into thick mud. Tiny Sea Monkeys swarmed over it and the ball became part of its chest, bulging out like a red-stitched goiter.

A range of expressions rippled across the creature's body, none of them happy. This was followed by a fierce cry as individual Monkeys raised their squealing voices together in triumph. Jerry shivered, the sound reminding him of a growling junkyard dog that's broken its leash and is about to make the most of unchecked freedom.

The monster took another step toward them, and the boys screamed.

"Run!"

They raced to the front door and flung it open, escape beckoning in the hallway beyond. The monster followed, each step a wet squish on the floor, like a series of underwater farts.

Their flight was cut short; Odie, the landlord, blocked the way, jangling keys in one hand while he pounded at a neighbor's door. A stack of moving boxes towered beside him, and Jerry recognized the signs of eviction. Odie stood between them and the staircase at the end of the hall.

The brothers shouted at him, babbling incoherently over each other. *"Look out!"* . . . *"Run! . . . Get away! . . . It's coming! . . . Oh-my-God, it's right behind us!"*

Odie whirled at them, confused. The boys' panic was infectious, and he almost joined in making tracks, as most people do when someone runs at them, screaming to flee for your life. But he took hold of himself, hell-bent to not let any snotty kids tell *him* what to do.

"You brats keep your voices down, and no running in the hallway!"

Luke shoved past him, but as Jerry followed, Odie reached out and snagged him by the back of his shirt collar.

"I said, *no running*," Odie repeated. It took a moment to recognize Jerry, but then he added with a toothy smirk, "And tell your mother I'll be expecting her at my place tonight. Rent's due again."

His smirk changed to a muttering laugh, *heh-heh-heh*, like an old cat coughing up hairballs.

Odie had turned his back to the apartment doors when he grabbed Jerry, who jerked in his arms.

"Let me go!" Jerry yelled. Jerry saw *it* coming from behind the landlord's back.

The creature had escaped their apartment and advanced down the hall, seeming to have mastered soggy ambulation. Strange things morphed from it, toys and weapons, as if the monster was cycling through available tools in a Swiss Army knife. Its squirming mass extended plastic airplane wings, and it seemed happy with this choice as it leapt into the air, gliding at them.

The flickering lights overhead reflected the sparkles of glass shards embedded in the Sea Monkey-monster, which also reflected in Jerry's wide eyes.

Odie saw that reflection and spun around.

The creature slammed into Odie's face, and glass shards pierced him. He tried to scream, but the rubbery beast wrapped around his face in a glob, suffocating him in jellied, pulsating brine shrimp.

Odie fell to the floor and rolled across the hallway, muffling wails like drowning under swamp ice. Sea Monkeys swarmed over his head, stretching against their gelatin walls as resolute as tree roots, trying to encase him like they did the baseball.

Luke came back up the staircase for his brother and froze, both watching Odie and the Sea Monkeys struggle against each other... Odie did not win.

The Sea Monkey creature stretched its blob-mass as far as elasticity would allow, reaching down the landlord's torso. It then tried crawling backward along the floor, fighting to drag Odie away. But Odie was just too fat to be encased entirely by the Monkey-monster and too heavy to be dragged off. The creature retracted its tendrils, returning to its original aquarium-shaped form, and unglued itself from the landlord.

It alternated panting in exhaustion and hissing at the boys.

"Don't move," Luke whispered to Jerry.

Luke crept to the door Odie had stood at moments before. He took one of the moving boxes and tip-toed toward the creature. Faster than Jerry thought possible, Luke leapt and threw the box over it, trapping the beast underneath. "Now! Help me!"

The brothers wrestled the box as it bounced violently across the floor. They managed to close up each side flap, containing the Sea Monkey-monster within, and carried it back to their apartment, leaving Odie's body sprawled in the hall.

They set the box on the table, and it shook for several minutes, while the creature fought for a way out; Jerry prayed the triple-ply, thick cardboard was sufficient to hold a murderous, drug-fueled Sea Monkey-monster within.

"What's going to happen when it gets out?" Jerry whispered.

"Man, I don't know," Luke replied. "But we've gotta get rid of it before Mom finds out."

"I wish I'd never ordered those crappy Sea Monkeys," Jerry said.

He happened to look over and see, lying on the floor, a crumpled instruction pamphlet and company guarantee.

That night the cops came and went, citing Odie's death as some random mugging-turned-murder. No one mourned him, and Sharon muttered something about *karma*.

The next day while she was at one of her three jobs, the postman carried away a triple-ply cardboard box marked: *Return to Sender.*

Inside, Jerry had slipped a note of paper, written upon in neat block letters.

I am not 100% satisfied with my Sea Monkey purchase. Please accept returned item and refund my dollar and thirty cents. Thank you.

Captain Pistachio's Charming Rampage

Jeff Strand

"I'm hungry!" said Frankie. "I want a snack! I want a candy bar!"

"I'm hungry too!" said Debbie. "I want a snack! I want ice cream!"

"What's a mother to do?" asked Mildred. "A busy parent like me doesn't have time to serve a candy bar to one child and ice cream to the other, and that gourmet ice cream with little chunks of candy in it is too expensive for our middle-class budget. I guess one of my children will have to resent me."

Mildred sat down at the kitchen table and wept. She always hated to see the disappointment in their young eyes. And though it was unfair to Debbie, she'd offer candy bars instead of ice cream. Frankie, at six, was already showing signs of becoming a serial killer and Mildred wanted to give him as idyllic a childhood as possible before he snapped.

"Don't be sad!" said an upbeat voice that she didn't recognize. "Why not give them delicious and nutritious *pistachios*?"

There was a stranger in the kitchen. A man—no, a nut! A man made of giant, unshelled pistachios. He was naked except for his tri-cornered hat, though since he had no genitalia Mildred felt comfortable that he wasn't a sexual predator. Actually, although a man made of pistachios should've fueled a million nightmares, he seemed like a charming, delightful fellow.

"Piss-tash-ee-ohs?" asked Frankie, stumbling over the word in an adorable way.

"That's right! Candy bars are just empty calories! Ice cream hurts if you have sensitive teeth! But pistachios are a salty, delicious treat with only 691 calories per cup! Chunky children like you should think about these things!"

"But I want ice cream!" whined Debbie.

The pistachio man smiled. His mouth looked like it had been drawn on his face with magic marker, so Mildred wasn't sure how it was able to move. Sorcery, she supposed.

"What if I were to tell you that pistachios are a hundred times better than ice cream?"

Debbie narrowed her eyes. Mildred hoped she didn't call the pistachio man a liar to his face.

"Who are you, exactly?" Mildred asked, to diffuse the tension.

"Why, I'm Captain Pistachio! I break into people's homes to show them that there are better snacking options! What are your names, little ones?"

"I'm Frankie."

"I'm Debbie."

"I already knew that," said Captain Pistachio. "I just didn't want to make you uneasy. So, Frankie and Debbie, I've got a special surprise for you!" He held up his hands, which were pistachio shells that opened and closed like the claws of a lobster. "Put out your hands!"

The children put out their hands. Captain Pistachio shook some pistachios into their palms.

"I don't like nuts," said Frankie.

"You only *think* you don't! These aren't peanuts, or walnuts, or any of those ghetto nuts. Pistachios are the best nuts of them all! Try 'em!"

"Go ahead, children," said Mildred.

Frankie and Debbie reluctantly popped the handfuls of pistachios into their mouths. They slowly began to chew. Frankie smiled. Then Debbie smiled.

"I love pistachios!" said Frankie.

"Me too!" said Debbie.

"I knew you would, kids!" said Captain Pistachio. He winked at Mildred with one of his drawn-on eyes. "Pistachios are scrumptious and they're good for you! So the next time you're in the mood for a tasty snack, what are you going to ask for?"

"*Pistachios!*" they both shouted.

"Thaaaaat's right! Yum, yum, yum! Well, it's time for Captain Pistachio to go now! I'll tell Santa you were good!" Captain Pistachio waved to the children as he walked toward the living room.

"One question," said Mildred.

"Sure! Captain Pistachio loves to answer questions!"

"You're made out of pistachios, right?"

"I certainly am!"

"Then is it really in your best interest to tell people to eat pistachios?"

Captain Pistachio frowned. "What do you mean?"

"I wouldn't go around encouraging children to eat human flesh. That would be insane, right?"

"Very."

"So isn't encouraging the consumption of pistachios equally insane?"

"I've never... I don't think so. I mean, if you go to a barbecue restaurant, there's usually a merry-looking pig on the sign. Nobody questions the pig's motives."

"Well, the pig isn't in my kitchen speaking to my family. If a magical pig showed up and said, 'Hi, I'm Captain Hammy, why not try a delicious strip of bacon?' yeah, I'd think it was bizarre."

"It's not like I cracked open my chest and invited them to start munching away."

"I apologize," said Mildred. "I've clearly offended you and that wasn't my intention."

"You didn't offend me," said Captain Pistachio. "You just made me see things differently is all. I've been telling kids to eat pistachios since the late 1970s. Nobody ever pointed out that it was cannibalism."

"I didn't say it was cannibalism. I didn't say that at all. *You've* never eaten a pistachio, have you?"

"Goodness, no!"

"So, then, it's not cannibalism."

Captain Pistachio wiped some cartoon sweat off his

brow. "Thank God. I thought I was a deviant."

"Well, you're still kind of a deviant," said Mildred. "Your whole message should be to discourage the public from eating pistachios. Why would you ever want people to eat them?"

"Because they're delicious and nutritious."

"But you're a pistachio!"

"I'm a magical pistachio man. A regular bag of pistachios purchased from your local supermarket doesn't have consciousness or a sense of identity. It doesn't know it's being eaten. It doesn't care. It's a goddamn nut!"

"Please don't curse in my home," said Mildred.

"I'm sorry," said Captain Pistachio. "That was completely inappropriate. I didn't realize I even knew that word. I just feel like you're attributing a sense of self-loathing to me that simply doesn't exist. A magical pistachio man can promote the nutritional value of pistachios without it being a cry for help."

Mildred nodded. "I was wrong. You've been doing this for a long time and don't need some frumpy housewife questioning your motives. Thank you for the pistachio samples you gave my children and I wish you the best of luck."

Captain Pistachio smiled. "Sure thing! Remember, when you want a tasty treat, you can't go wrong with pistachios! They're the yummiest!"

"Bye, Captain Pistachio!" said Frankie and Debbie.

"Bye, kids! I'll tell the Easter Bunny you said hi!"

"I'm sorry—one more question," said Mildred.

"What?"

"When you opened your hand-shells and poured nuts into their hands, where did those come from?"

"I beg your pardon?"

"Had you been carrying them the whole time?"

"I still don't get what you're asking."

"Now that I've had a chance to think about it, it just seems odd that you didn't bring a bag of pistachios. Why would you pour them out of your hands like that? Where did they come from?"

Captain Pistachio glared at her. "Are you accusing me of excreting pistachios?"

"From your hands? God, no!"

"Wait, that's not what I meant. Are you accusing me of secreting pistachios?"

"No. I wasn't accusing you of anything. It was a simple question. Where did the pistachios come from?"

"If you offered a handful of nuts to my children, I wouldn't suggest that they were produced by *your* body."

"I'm not a giant anthropomorphic nut."

"The answer is no, my body does not produce pistachios, okay?" Captain Pistachio held up his hands. "See these? To you, they may look like some grotesque deformity, something a soldier might have attached to the bloody stumps of his wrists after he gets his hands blown off in combat. To me, they're normal, because I'm a fucking magical pistachio man. Hands made of pistachio shells are very convenient for carrying around pistachios. So you can just suck my salty, unshelled dick, lady."

"Frankie, Debbie, go upstairs," said Mildred, backing away from the angry pistachio man.

"No! The kids stay where they are! I came here to offer you a healthy snacking alternative, to make life a little easier for you, but instead you act like I'm some depraved freak with a self-cannibalism fetish! Do you think it's easy to be Captain Pistachio? Do you think I get to go out and have normal social outings? Do you think I've ever felt the sensual touch of a woman? All I do is go around giving my little performance for ungrateful hags like you! Would it kill your moon-faced kids to eat a piece of broccoli every once in a while? Nooooo, all they want is candy and ice cream, so I'm here to offer something that'll keep the spoiled little shits from having temper tantrums!"

"Frankie, Debbie, go upstairs *now*!" Mildred shouted. "Run! Lock your bedroom door!"

Frankie and Debbie fled the kitchen, screaming.

"That was your worst mistake yet," said Captain Pistachio, stepping in front of the doorway between the kitchen and living room. "The only thing keeping you alive is that I would never murder a mother in front of her children, but there's nothing stopping me now!"

Mildred ran for the back door. She frantically turned the knob. The door wouldn't open.

"It's no use," said Captain Pistachio with a cartoon sneer. "I've already barricaded it."

"But why?"

"Do you think I'm greeted with universal adoration? Sometimes when families see me they freak the fuck out. I can't have the people calling the cops about an intruder in a giant pistachio costume, now, can I?"

"It's a costume?"

Captain Pistachio shook his head. "No. But when people see me, their first assumption is that I'm a guy in a costume. I mean, that was your first thought, right? Your brain went to 'guy in costume' before 'giant living pistachio creature,' right?"

Mildred said nothing.

Captain Pistachio smiled so widely that his magic-marker mouth stretched beyond the borders of his face and the edges floated in mid-air. But then the smile disappeared, and he gazed at her with true hatred. "I've killed a lot of people, Mildred. A *lot* of people. My soul is a dark abyss. Whenever I close my eyes, I see rivers of blood, and I see the screaming faces of my countless victims being carried away in the crimson current. I am haunted, Mildred. So very haunted."

"I could put you out of your misery," Mildred offered.

"Bitch, I didn't say I was suicidal. If I wanted to die, I'd just pry my head open." Captain Pistachio frowned, as if regretting making a comment about how easily he could be killed.

Mildred ran at him, arms outstretched.

Captain Pistachio slammed his open hand into her chest. The sharp ends of his shells sank deep into her warm, tender flesh. Mildred cried out in pain but did not fall. Captain Pistachio stabbed her with his other hand. He stared into her eyes, loving the expression of terror, waiting for that glorious moment when the light in her eyes would fade as sweet death consumed her.

She spat bloody saliva into his face, defiant.

Then she grabbed his head with both hands.

"*Noooo!*" he cried. Yeah, blabbing about his weakness had indeed been poor strategy.

She pried the shell apart, and both halves fell to the floor, leaving a desiccated, light green pistachio exposed. It had cloudy eyes with a milky substance leaking from them, two slits for a nose, and a thin, uneven mouth.

"*Don't look at me!*" Captain Pistachio wailed. "*Avert your cursed gaze!*"

But Mildred couldn't look away. The face under the shell wasn't charming. It was nightmarish. She would never have let this monster feed pistachios to her children if she'd seen his true visage.

Mildred leaned forward and took a bite out of his face. A pistachio was softer than a peanut, and it put up little resistance.

"*Stop it! Stop—*"

Mildred tore his mouth off with her own, cutting off his scream. She chewed his mouth and swallowed. Then she ate away at the top of his head, hoping to devour his brain.

Captain Pistachio fell to the floor. He lay there, unmoving. Dead.

"Burn in hell," Mildred told him. She didn't know if magical pistachio men went to hell, but wherever he was, she hoped an eternity of suffering awaited him.

She could hear her blood dripping onto the tile floor. Her wounds were fairly serious, but she was pretty sure she had a while before she bled to death. She'd scoop a bowl of ice cream for Debbie and find a candy bar for Frankie, and then she'd drive herself to the hospital.

Your Diabolical Baby

Santiago Eximeno

Translated into English by Alicia L. Alonso

A practical book by Martha Ferber

Author's Prologue

I won't accept a god who'd let a mother find her baby dead on her hip when there was food in her hand that might have saved it!
—John Brunner, *The Sheep Look Up*

Dear friend, this book you are now holding in your hands is your gateway to the wonderful world of maternity. This book will be both support and solace for you, and I hope it leads you with a loving hand (and also an iron fist, since from this day forward determination must be your companion) along the road of your journey with your diabolical baby.

If there's anything I've learned these past two years after birthing, raising, and giving unto darkness half a dozen offspring, it is that we, as women and mothers, feel very much alone the first time our newborn baby looks up at us with its bloodshot eyes. That is the reason why I wish to share my experiences with you, in the hope they will be a soothing inspiration, helping you live this wonderful new life as fully as possible with your satanic baby by your side.

A big hug from Hell,
Martha.

Editor's Introduction

This small book, practically a brochure, represents one of the greatest personal satisfactions we, as editors, have ever felt. For years, we came across a number of virgin young ladies that, upon finding out they were pregnant, would frantically rush to their doctor's office. Confused and disturbed by an event that escaped their understanding, these young ladies often endangered their offspring's life, forcing all of us who are part of Darkness to deal with them in rather unpleasant ways. This is why a book like Martha Ferber's is a breeze of stale air for our Community, a necessary message of love for many concubines of Darkness who, having forgotten—and occasionally not even knowing—about their obligations regarding the creature that lurked in their womb, attempted to abort one of the most beautiful moments that a servant of the Night could ever experience.

Let these words pay homage to a book that, with pleasant and familiar words, restores Darkness to the act of creating life—Darkness that light tried to snatch away over the past centuries.

Author's Introduction

Dear ladies: I have decided to divide this book into three

chapters, and each of these chapters into six sections. I firmly believe that three times six offers the vision of what I wish to tell you in an educational, clear, and concise manner. Read this book from start to finish if you wish, or skip to the chapter of your choice and use it as a manual. Whatever you do, enjoy your reading. And remember: everything we do, we do for Him.

Chapter I: Something Is Growing Inside You

Yes, my friend. You wake up one morning and you feel like throwing up. You also feel tired and a bit queasy. When you go outside, it seems like the sunlight wants to burn your skin. Aren't these enough signs?

We often assume that we know what goes on inside our bodies. But when the evidence flutters around us like a plague of locusts, it's sometimes hard to accept reality. Ladies, do not fear. We've all been through the same thing. We were all afraid the first time it happened and we didn't know what to do. If you speak to your girlfriends or your neighbors, or even to your human mate, they will all offer you advice. But let me warn you here and now: they are wrong. Do not go to your doctor as soon as you discover the symptoms. First, seek help within your circle and put things in order.

"But," you ask, "what happens to those of us who find ourselves abandoned, far away from the people who can help us at a time like this?" It is for you, my friends, that I have written this small book, which I hope will lead you step by step into this new life of service to He Who Does Not Forgive.

Your Baby

Many of you will ask yourselves: "Is the baby I carry in my womb diabolical?" Dear friends, most of the time this is an absurd question. Many of you have ridden naked on the back of large black wolves with your skin doused in oil. Some of you have received in your own bedroom the visit of the Billy goat and have let him pour his seed into your torn innards. Or perhaps you've mated with a coyote in an abandoned desert. I understand that those of you who were raped by an incubus or seduced in dreams by minor demons (the so-called "Rosemary Syndrome", very common throughout the past century) may have doubts. Still, you cannot simply wait for the creature to be born and look at you with its blood-red eyes to know what it's all about. The correct thing to do is to have previously taken certain steps to confirm that what grows inside you is indeed an offspring of Darkness.

During pregnancy, your baby reacts to external stimuli just as any other baby would. Stroke your belly from the start, and observe the baby's reactions. Its movements can be indicators of many more things than you can imagine. Six weeks after conception, moisten your finger with your own vaginal discharge and then draw an inverted cross on your skin, starting a few inches below your breasts and ending at your belly button. If your baby is diabolical, you will feel a sudden jolt of pleasure cursing through your body, an orgasm of cataclysmic proportions. As weeks go by and its size increases, you will feel its presence with an ever-greater force. Draw a pentagram on your skin, around your belly button. You will see the moving shape of the baby's hands, drawing from the inside the same lines you've drawn on the outside.

You

Treat your pregnancy calmly and lovingly. As you know, the most important thing is the child. You are nothing but a recipient for the Seed of Evil, as dispensable as an old flower vase or a broken-down piece of furniture. This, however, doesn't mean that you must abuse yourself or set your personal care aside, since the safe arrival of this new incarnation of the Dark to our reality depends on you.

Stick to your usual diet and habits, and add small details to help the child grow correctly. For example, before you go to sleep drink a bit of absinthe. If that's hard to find where you live, then try drinking something with high alcohol content, one or two glasses a night. Smoke a cigar or a few cigarettes, but only at night, and swallow the smoke. Sex, of course, is essential. If you have a steady partner, try to set up meetings with third parties in hotel rooms. You will find ads in the paper for those who enjoy being with pregnant women. In any case, what you must certainly do is masturbate daily.

Your Family

My dear lady friends, it's quite possible that some of you might have a steady partner. We will cover that in the next chapter, since it's important to make a decision after the birth. However, during your pregnancy you must behave naturally towards him, see to his wishes and pleasure him if necessary. As to the rest of your family, treat them with courtesy and let them participate in your pregnancy. Do not fear for the child, because when the moment comes you will walk away from them.

It could be that some members of your family follow a religious belief that is not compatible with your pregnancy. Those are the ones you must keep close by, for their fragile faith will tremble when they are around you. Let them approach you; invite them to caress your belly. Excite them. Soon enough they will feel so uncomfortable around you that you will never see them again. If at any moment you feel that they might suspect what you are really carrying inside your womb, then try to hurt them or even end their life. Just as long as you can do it in such a way that seems accidental.

Your Friends

Throughout the years, many women have managed to restrict their circle of friends to an essential minimum. Man, being a childish creature dominated by his sexual impulses, needs his equals in order to create a social framework where he can see himself reflected. A woman, however, is capable of limiting her need for love, and thus her dependency.

As positive as a reduced circle of intimate girlfriends might be, it can also be negative, since intimate friends are stronger and more tenacious. They'll call you. They'll want to see you and give you advice. They'll want to be by your side, or even hug you and stroke your bulging belly. Let them do it. Let them trust you. Afterwards you can shrewdly try to get rid of them. You know how to do it. After all, you're a woman like us. Seduce their men, humiliate them in public by cruelly criticizing their most intimate flaws. It will certainly hurt you, since they were your friends, but it is your duty to cut off all the false links binding you to useless earthly passions once the Redemptor has blessed you with His Seed.

Your Doctor

Maybe you're one of those fearful and insecure women who've never been to the doctor. It's also possible that you're the type of woman who trusts her good old gynecologist. In any case, we recommend that you handle this pregnancy with an unknown doctor unrelated to you or to your family, someone who will treat you like a number and not like a person. That way it will be easier for you to make your own decisions and avoid certain compromises that, should you have a close relationship with your doctor, you would otherwise be forced to accept.

Your Circle

Are you a concubine of the Dark? Then your artfulness must have led you to the nearest circle, a group of men and women yearning to bring to life a new servant of pain and suffering. I imagine you meet every Saturday and practice everything that satisfies you, without fear of what others might say. Congratulations! They will be by your side and help you with everything you need, especially on those occasions when you feel faint and it might be necessary to infuse some firmness into your decisions.

It is also possible, my friend, that you're a solitary woman who only had marginal contact with the diabolical, and it hasn't been until now that you have started to interact with The Other Side. In that case, learn fast from those around you. If you don't know anyone, then remember that we live in the information era; if you have a copy of this book in your hands, it should not be too hard to find others like you.

Chapter II: The Redemptor Is Born

Yes, my friend, the moment you've been waiting for during the past nine months has arrived. Throughout this time you've felt the offspring inside you moving and caressing you. You have enjoyed him and he has enjoyed you. You know that, no matter how much you'd like to, you cannot keep him inside you any longer, and the time has come to let him come out into the open and face this realm of reality. In this chapter we shall discuss all that, as well as all those little things that make your offspring so special.

His Name

The name you freely choose for your child will define his spirit and free the gift inside him. For that reason, it is of capital importance that you choose a correct and adequate name. In the past, when registrars demanded names of saints, we were forced to use inadequate, obscenely perverse names that referred to our enemy. This diminished the strength of our dark children. My dear friend, I shall not suggest a name for your offspring in this book, since it must be a completely free choice, but I must ask you to stay away from names that, in one extreme or another, will not help his inner growth. Namely: you should not call him Baal, but neither should you use the perverse name of our enemy's sacrificed son.

Birth

Everything is ready for the birth. The light of the full moon will be your guide. Stay relaxed when you go to the hospital by controlling your blood pressure the way you know so well. It's normal for women carrying human children in their womb to give in to pain; do not try to be an exception. Do not give away who you are, for a servant of our enemy might be lurking behind a nurse's smiling face. If you haven't done so already, choose a hospital that will not separate the newborn from you at any time. It's important that, from his first moment, the child has contact with a corrupted and perverse soul like yours.

During birth you will feel pain, an inhuman pain that will eventually become a forbidden pleasure, a relentless orgasm of fire that will devour you from the inside. If you feel you might not be able to remain in control, ask for an epidural. It will limit your pleasure, but it will not in any way affect the Seed of Evil.

Once you are holding the newborn in your hands, smile at him. Do not fear. At first it will be hard, even for very observant people, to discover that an incarnation of the most impure horror lives and breathes amongst them.

Do not forget to consign the exact time of his birth, as you will need it later to confirm the exact time of the parting.

The First Steps

From the first moment of his birth, offer your breast. Breastfeeding will establish a bond between you, a union beyond the flesh that may save your soul on the day of the Apocalypse. You should keep in mind that his teeth will grow soon, before he's four months old, and they will be sharp. Breastfeeding will become painful. If you opt to wean, do not feel guilty. I did that myself with my first offspring.

A daily bath is not necessary, no matter how much mothers of human children might insist. In fact, it's even inappropriate for your child. Limit his baths to once a week, and always be careful with the temperature of the water. Keep your offspring near you as long as possible. Let him feel the warmth of your body and your skin, as well as your smell and taste and all that which, when he grows up, might help him identify you and not hurt you.

During the first few days you will receive many visits. Be unfriendly, reject them. They will use their small minds to fabricate the excuses you need in order to justify your behavior. Take advantage of that. This is also the right time to break up with your partner, if you still have one. Hurt him, make him feel guilty, do whatever it takes so he will accept your rejection. In any way possible, get rid of him. You do not need him.

The Small Details

There are hundreds of small details you must take into account in your everyday interactions with your child. Many of them will not really affect the way you care for him or the way he evolves, but they will help you to get to know your newborn better and empathize with him. Below is a short list of trivia and details you must take into account. No doubt, they will be of great use to you:

- When the child looks over his shoulder to what seems to be empty space, he's actually looking at the face of his True Father.
- Whereas initially his eyes will be a faint gray color, they will eventually change to their usual, defini-

tive dark blood red.

☩ Do not try to understand the child's guttural sounds. He's pronouncing words in a language made for other types of throats.

☩ Do not worry when, as you pass near a church or any other place that exhibits pagan symbols, your child cries inconsolably.

☩ At times, while he sleeps, he will laugh in a way you will only be able to describe as diabolical.

☩ Clip his nails daily, because they will quickly grow sharp and hard.

☩ The bath water will boil if you submerge the child for longer than ten minutes.

☩ Avoid mirrors, for the child will be horrified when seeing his own reflection.

☩ Never, ever, ever caress his chin and say "Coo!".

Children, Mothers, Neighbors and Other Menaces

During his first months of life, the child will pique the curiosity of all those who cross your path. Once you leave the safety of your home, you will not have a moment's rest. That which you can control at home you will not be able to control on the street. Neighbors will approach you to meet the child. Young and old women will halt you, flashing hypocritical smiles, with the sole interest of looking at the newborn's face. Other mothers, armed with their own children, will suggest absurd exchanges of anecdotes, as if children unlike their own simply do not exist.

Let them approach you, but don't allow them to touch the child, even if that means you have to be nasty. Should a stranger touch him, remember to wash the area with vinegar as soon as you get home. Also, remember to curse the devious individual who dared lay his or her hand on the child. Curse them several times so that the child will hear you and, when he grows up, remember. No doubt, by then he will know what to do in order to restore balance.

The Gift

My friend, it's hard for me to define with one single word the power that your child will manifest once he reaches maturity, but for want of a better term let us call it the "gift." The gift will reveal itself at full power later on, when He is no longer with you, but it's possible that while he is at your side you might witness some relevant moments. There are cases of deaths—most of them will look like accidents—of people who come into contact with the child and, for reasons impossible for a mortal to understand, fall into disgrace. These cases are not rare. Whatever you see, try to accept it as something natural. Above everything, do not fear the child because he will never hurt you, at least not during these first few months.

Chapter III: The Preparation

Yes, my friend, the first few months have gone by and soon, very soon, the child you hold in your arms, smiling with a mouth full of teeth, will go his own way. It's necessary during this last month that you pay extra special attention, since you must make some essential arrangements for the child to become what he is meant to be.

In this chapter I will tell you about the signs you've already observed, the needs that must be seen to and that, perhaps, have already come up. Learn what you don't yet know and correct any mistakes you might have made. Everything will soon be over, and then it will be time to close all that was left open.

The Nanny

You must hire a nanny. Not one of those young girls who offer to look after children for one night, nor one of those agency women who charge by the hour. You must hire a nanny who will come to your home when the offspring is exactly three months, three days and three hours old. She will knock on your door and you will let her in. From that moment on she will live with you and take care of the offspring's education, the part of his education that you cannot provide. Also, should you wish, she will do whatever you want in order to pleasure you.

The Child's True Friends

The offspring is born, and it's time for him to spend time with his true friends. As you know, other children, even those who also carry the Seed of Evil in them, are not his friends. You, my dear friend, are his mother, the tool that enabled his entry into this world. But you will never be able to consider yourself his friend.

The child will seek friendship from two creatures that, once he's ready, will present themselves. They will be his companions for the rest of their lives, long enough for the young offspring to grow up and become a man. For that reason, when they come to your house, open the doors and let them in, let them come into contact with the child, let them play with him.

First it will be the dog. It will be large and black, and will never bark. If it ever sees the child in danger it will act, but otherwise it will try to go unnoticed. You need not worry about it. Just let it stay close to the child whenever necessary.

Next, the crow will arrive. It will be small and black, and it will never caw. It will remain at the window in the child's room, motionless, until the time for parting arrives. Ignore it; it will ignore you back.

The Last Week

You know there's a specific date on which you must say good-bye to the child. We will discuss that further on, but it's important that you take a special interest in the last week. With the help of the nanny the child has progressed along his path. But he needs you, his mother, to be there for one very important step: that of the blood.

Up until now, the child has fed on maternal milk and the concoctions the nanny suggested to you after his weaning. During this last week the child must taste blood, and he must do it with you. The first two or three days you can limit it to red meat. Buy juicy steaks at the market and serve them to the child, uncooked. Let him tear them apart with his teeth and enjoy the taste. He might vomit after the first few bites, but you shouldn't worry about it.

The next few days, let him taste your blood. Make small cuts in your arms in areas you can afterwards hide underneath your clothes. Then, let the child drink from the wounds and suck the flowing blood. Smile at all times, especially when he looks at you. Whatever happens, do not stop smiling. And, as you already know, if you need help with this stage the nanny will be happy to provide it.

Small Cruelties

You might witness some of the initiation rituals the nanny will teach the child. Do not be scandalized by it, and do not reproach the child. Think of it as small cruelties pertaining to his age. After all, who cares if someone tears off a live cat's skin or nails small agonized animals to the wall and waits for them to rot before eating them?

The Parting

There's a preset day and time for the parting: on the sixth month, the sixth day, six hours after the child's birth. That will be the exact moment when you must deliver the child. You will know because the dog will bark for the first time, the crow will fly out the window and the nanny will commit suicide. This last event might be uncomfortable for you, since you'll need to get rid of the body afterwards. But don't worry: the nanny will give you the tools and explain to you what to do with her corpse before she hangs herself.

At the exact moment of parting, two old men will knock at your door. Give them the child without asking any questions. Do not say good-bye. He will not even look back.

And Now What?

My friend, whether you want to or not, everything will be over. Whereas He Who No Longer Belongs To You will grow up and spread horror among those who—blind and naive—dare consider themselves his equals, it is your duty to start off on a new path in the crusade that is your life. Your possible options can be summarized as three:

+ Become a recipient of the Seed of Evil, which will allow you to again enjoy an indescribable experience, but which is not without risk, since there are not few cases of mothers that have been devoured from the inside by their second or third offspring.
+ Join your circle and welcome newcomers. This will, presumably allow you to stay in contact—marginal, but contact still—with He Who Is No Longer Your Son and others like Him.
+ Live your new life and enjoy the pleasures of the flesh that this reality permits, until He Who Is No Longer Your Son comes to claim your soul.

Whatever you decide, my dear, I would like to personally thank you in the name of all of Them, and wish you the best. Thank you, my friend. Without you, none of this would be possible.

I will see you in Hell,
Martha Ferber

The Night Stockers

Sean Logan

It all started with Jahn's dreadlocks. The problem was not that he *had* dreadlocks, even though he was a white kid with wealthy parents. That was a different problem. This problem was that his dreadlocks were so dense and oily that they made an ideal environment through which the alien virus could travel.

The virus was attracted to the brain waves of intelligent mammals. Even though Jahn was not considered intelligent by human standards, the neurons in his brain did fire at a sufficient level to attract the virus, which had rested dormant in the Spendthrift Drug and Discount stockroom until Jahn sneaked to the pet food aisle to smoke marijuana from a homemade pipe he'd fashioned from an empty Soul Crusher Energy Drink can. As Jahn sucked in a lungful of smoke, he leaned back against a forty-pound bag of Dainty Dog dog food, which had been slouching in the back of that aisle for nearly five years.

The origin of the virus is unknown, but it reached our planet on a meteor that crushed the skull of an unsuspecting beef cow as it was being transported from feedlot 12B at the GenChem Farming Complex in Winona, Texas to the United Beef Processing Center in Lubbock. The nearly headless cow was processed and shipped to the Pet Food, Baby Laxative and Industrial Lubricants division of Amalgamated Products Corporation, where a small portion was combined with peanut hulls, blood meal, bone phosphate, rendered swine fat, and a wide range of additional binders, coloring agents and preservatives, and packaged as Dainty Dog Fancy Chow with Real Beef.

Five years later, Jahn leaned against one of those bags and a greasy clump of his hair slipped into a small tear in the packaging. The virus attached itself to the matted blond cluster and began moving slowly toward his brain. This process would take two weeks. It was also two weeks until the night of the store's inspection.

Dirk parked his '86 Camaro in the back of the Spendthrift parking lot. He looked in the rearview, combed his shoulder-length blond hair and straightened his mustache. He was looking good. What he looked like was a wrestler. And he had the guns for that shit. He was packing an extra forty pounds, maybe, but when he sucked it in, he looked like a goddamn wrestler. And if he was a wrestler, he thought he'd probably call himself the Big Kahuna, because with his blond hair he also looked like a big wave-surfing beach stud.

This is your night, big guy, he said to himself. *You get that stockroom in shape, show the district manager you know how to get things done around here, and no more of this assistant manager bullshit. No more making fifteen measly-ass dollars an hour. You'll be a full-on store manager—making eighteen dollars an hour. Get 'er done!*

Dirk flexed both his cannons and threw a punch at his rearview, snapping the mirror off its frame and into the passenger seat. *God damn it!* Whatever. He could Crazy Glue that shit tomorrow. He had more important business. That stockroom was standing between him and his promotion like some bitch-ass dragon. And tonight, he was a dragon slayer.

Dirk got out of the car and threw on his orange polyester vest. His crew was already waiting by the door, and damn, he was stuck with a sorry group—two lazy teenage stockboys and one grizzled old hag.

"How's it hanging, ladies?"

Jahn was smoking a clove cigarette and scratching at his dreadlocks. "I'm not a lady."

"Well, Erma here may look like Merle Haggard, but she is technically a lady."

"Up yours," Erma said around the cigarette dangling from her thin lips. She plucked it out and flicked it into the parking lot.

Chester was slumped against the door, his belly heaped in front of him like a pile of dirty laundry, his finger knuckle-deep in his right nostril. "Chester," Dirk said, snapping his fingers at him like a dog, "are you picking your nose?"

"Certainly not!" Chester said, extracting his finger and trying to look indignant. "I just had an itch."

"What, on your brain? Come on, up and at 'em." Dirk unlocked the front door and led the troops past the cash registers and down aisle one to the stockroom. "Okay, huddle up."

The three of them slouched and moaned and eye-rolled into a circle. Dirk leaned in and put his arms around their shoulders. "All right, you all know Mrs. Windbone has been out on disability since that case of Man-E-Pedi Nail Polish fell on her foot. Well, I just heard she's not coming back. That puts yours truly in a primo position for head honcho around here. But if we don't get this stockroom cleaned and organized before Mr. Crastfinger gets here—"

"Whoa," Jahn said, "you don't think we're going to get the whole stockroom done *tonight*, do you?"

"Hell yeah we are," Dirk said. "Mr. Crastfinger gets here at five tomorrow morning, so we've got six hours to get this place perfect."

"Hey, if you're going to be the new manager, can I get paid time off for a Eugene Marley concert next month?" Jahn asked. "He's Bob Marley's third cousin. And also could I smoke pot in the break room? It's technically part of my religion."

"Well I don't think I could really allow—"

"He won't be able to do shit," Erma said.

"Oh yes I will. And I know how to take care my friends."

"Must we continue huddling?" Chester asked. "My back's beginning to spasm."

"Okay, fine," Dirk said. "Let's just get this done, all right? Please?"

They broke up the huddle. Chester leaned backward, grimacing and rubbing at his lower back. "I think I should lie in repose for a moment to let my vertebrae realign."

"Oh for the love of God," Dirk said. "Just get to work, all right? I'm going to check on the back rooms."

The three of them shuffled into the stockroom and Dirk went back to the men's room, where some joker had used the seat for target practice. He pulled a few paper towels from the dispenser, and when he did, he caught a look at himself in the mirror. He'd only been on the job a few minutes, but already he wasn't feeling like such a hot beach stud. He was feeling like an overweight forty-two-year-old wearing a name tag and wiping up piss. He needed to catch a break. If he got that store manager gig, that was something he could be proud of. It wasn't like being a running back for the Niners or playing drums for White Snake, but if he saw an old friend from high school, he wouldn't be too embarrassed to say he was head manager of East Billingham's largest drugstore.

But the kid was right. There was no way in hell they were going to get that stockroom done before Mr. Crastfinger got there. It was hopeless.

Dirk flexed his guns in the mirror. It made him feel better, but only a little.

At a quarter after two, Jahn was halfway finished organizing the stockroom's cosmetics aisle when he felt a sudden, sharp pain in his scalp, like he'd been stabbed with an ice pick. The pain was replaced by a queasy warmth that spread quickly across the top of his head, and then it was gone.

The skin beneath one of his dreads was already swollen and itchy. He didn't want to go to the hospital because he didn't believe in Western medicine, but he could go home and smoke some ganja. If he was going to die of a brain aneurysm, he wanted to be high for it.

But, no, he needed the money. He had to save up for his senior trip to Jamaica. They were going to stay at a sweet all-inclusive resort. And he'd probably get a chance to hang with some of his Rastafarian brothers and sisters on the island. But his cheap-ass parents weren't even going to pay for his plane ticket. They *were* going to get him a BMW for graduation, but only a 3 Series.

He also needed money for ganja. He'd been smoking extra the last two days to deal with his itchy scalp. It didn't make it less itchy, but it did make him forget about it occasionally. The problem was that he could scratch *around* the clump of hair, but he couldn't scratch *inside* of it. Although sometimes it helped to pull on it, so he did... and the dreadlock came off in his hand.

"What the hey!" Jahn yelled. He looked at the rope of hair and scabbed end that had detached from his scalp. He touched his scalp and felt a hole the width of the lock, about the size of a quarter. "What the hecking hey!"

Jahn felt around the hole. It didn't hurt much, just a slight sting on the outer surface. Inside was rough and hard, about a half inch deep and spongy in the middle. "Wait a minute," Jahn mumbled as a sick horror washed over him. "That's not…that's not…that's not my *brain*?!"

Jahn felt like he was having an out-of-body experience as he stumbled out of the cosmetics aisle toward the other end of the stockroom where Chester was breaking down cardboard boxes.

Hello? said a voice. It must have been on the store intercom, but it sounded like someone was talking straight into his ear.

Testing, testing, one, two, three. Jahn spun around, expecting to see someone leaning over his shoulder. The voice was definitely not coming from the scratchy old intercom. It sounded like it was practically coming from inside his head.

You do hear us, don't you, Jahn?

Jahn couldn't see where the voice was coming from. "Where are you?"

We're inside you now.

"What?! What did you say?"

You're going to have to remain calm, Jahn. We can't have you calling attention to yourself.

"You're inside my head?! HOLY SH—"

Jahn fell to his knees as a debilitating pain stabbed him in the eyes. Two years ago, he was pepper-sprayed by a stubby security guard as he staged a sit-in in his principal's office to protest non-dolphin-safe tuna being used in the cafeteria (which he later discovered was untrue). He thought that had hurt, but it was nothing compared to the ungodly pain searing his eyeballs now.

The pain vanished.

Do we have your attention, Jahn? You're going to have to remain calm and not call attention to yourself.

"What do you mean, you're inside me?" Jahn whimpered. "Who are you?"

You can think of us as a virus if you like. We entered through the top of your head and we are replicating inside your cells right now.

"You're a virus? But how are you talking to me? You know English?"

No, you know English. We transmit thoughts collectively that your brain translates into words you understand.

"I don't get it."

It doesn't matter whether you get it or not. That is what's happening.

"So, who's talking. Are you the one in charge?"

We are all talking. Or, rather, we are all communicating. The voice you hear is something that was already inside you. We are the thoughts behind the voice, but not the voice itself.

Jahn realized that the voice was that of Mr. Chubb, his fourth period metal shop teacher. "What happens now? I don't want you in my head."

We're going to stay.

Jahn pictured a microscopic version of bald, mustachioed Mr. Chubb inside his head saying this.

"For how long?"

For the rest of your life.

"No way!"

Don't worry, it won't be for very long. You'll be dead soon.

"WHAT?!"

More searing pain, this time in his sinuses. It felt like he'd snorted a habanero pepper.

The pain vanished.

We told you, you have to remain calm.

Jahn felt lightheaded, a clammy tingling on the back of his neck. "I'm sorry. But did you say ...did you say I'll be—"

Dead soon. Yes, you'll be dead soon. Our preliminary data suggests about six hours. As we said, we're replicating in your cells right now. When we're released from the cells, they are destroyed. It's an unavoidable side effect. It's really nothing personal.

"But I'm going to—"

Watch the volume, Jahn.

"Sorry," he said more quietly. "But how can I not take it personally? You said I'm going to die. There's nothing more personal than that."

You can look at it that way if you choose. It's not important. What is important is that you help us proliferate. We need to spread to another organism before your body dies.

"You want me to help you? Even though you're going to kill me?"

Thumbs in his eyes, icepicks in his ears, habaneros in his nose.

The pain vanished, leaving Jahn dazed and breathless. "Please, please, please stop doing that."

It will only get worse, Jahn. As we map the details of your body, our ability to control you will only grow. Eventually we'll have complete control, but for now we have to convince you to help us by threatening you with immense pain. As we multiply, your body will decay. Before you're unable to move, we need you to help us spread into the body of another human. Your thoughts are telling us that you have a coworker named Chester.

"Yeah," Jahn said, poking gently inside the hole in his head, touching what might be his brain. "But how am I supposed to get you into his body?"

We can spread through direct contact with most bodily fluids. The easiest way will be to engage in an open-mouthed kiss with him.

"WHAT?!"

Jahn felt a cramping, tearing electricity rip through him, from the hole in his head to the tips of his fingers. He dropped to the stockroom's cement floor, contracting into the fetal position.

The pain vanished. "Please, for the love of Zion, I'll do what you want. I can't take anymore."

That's good, Jahn. And we think it would be best if you got started right away. We aren't familiar with human courtship rituals, but we imagine it could take time, particularly for two heterosexual males.

"Yeah, you're not kidding. I hope you guys appreciate what I'm doing for you."

We do, Jahn. We do.

Chester Orillius Lancaster III pulled his mighty sword from its sheath. She was called Persephone for the dread queen of the Underworld, and she had vanquished countless enemies on the fields of war. She had served Chester well, the muse to his deathly arts. But that day the two faced an adversary with such cunning, with such a vampiric taste for blood that their mettle would surely be tested. But if Chester could summon all his battle-forged strength, and if Persephone could strike good and true, then victory may once again be their fate.

Chester raised his boxcutter and sliced along the taped seam of the empty Baby Angel Bath Tissue box. He folded his cardboard foe and threw it atop the others like so many fallen warriors.

"Hey, Chester." It was Jahn, looking sweaty and pale.

"You're not looking well, Jahn," Chester said. "You're a bit peaked."

"Well, you're looking pretty good," Jahn said, raising his lips into a creepy smile. "You been working out?"

Chester thought about this, and yes, in fact, he had been. "I've been practicing the ancient art of Tai Chi Ch'uan in the park with my grandmother." He moved gracefully into his Step Back and Repulse the Monkey posture.

"That's great, that's really great," Jahn said, perspiration gathering in his eyebrows. "I thought you'd been looking especially fit lately. And what do you think of me, by the way? Do you think I'm a good-looking guy? Do you think girls might find a guy like me attractive?"

Chester thought about this, rubbing his smooth, round chin. "No, not especially."

Jahn flinched. He didn't seem to expect that reply.

"Really? You don't think I'm attractive?"

"Sadly, no. I mean, there is a certain pedestrian symmetry to your features that is consistent with traditional standards of…" Chester searched for right words, "…physical comeliness. But any positive qualities are offset by your matted hair. Really, Jahn, it makes you look like a vagabond, and frankly I find it frightening. And there's your smell."

Jahn's bottom lip quivered. "What do you mean? I don't smell."

"I'm afraid you do. You smell like my grandmother's food pantry, like mold and root vegetables. I'm sorry, but I just can't imagine any girl being attracted to someone who has clumpy hobo hair and smells like old rutabagas."

"But I've had lots of girlfriends!" Jahn cocked his head for a moment, like he was listening for something. His eyes brightened as if he'd thought of something clever. "Hey, do *you* have a girlfriend?"

"As a matter of fact, I do," Chester said, raising an eyebrow, feeling like a man of the world. "She's a fortieth level Mage in World of Warcraft."

Jahn seemed excited by this. "That's super. Really. Say, let me ask a question, from one guy to another: Have you kissed this lucky lady of yours?"

Chester's chin dipped just a bit. "Well, not as such. We've battled together on countless occasions, but we've yet to cross swords on the physical plane."

"So you haven't met in person yet?"

"No, but our time is near at hand. She'll be in town with

her parents next month to see *Arms Wide Open*, the Creed musical. We'll be going on a proper date then."

"Your first date, you must be nervous. That's a lot of pressure."

Chester hadn't really thought about that. He was just looking forward to meeting his fair maiden for the first time. "Why would I be nervous?"

Jahn looked surprised. "Why would you be nervous? Because it's your first date! That's when she'll size you up as a potential mate. If you don't come across like you know what you're doing, that's it. You do know what you're doing, don't you? I mean, you've kissed girls before."

Chester lowered his head, glancing up at Jahn. "No," he said quietly.

"No?"

"I've been saving myself for someone special. You don't think she'd hold that against me, do you?"

Jahn rolled his eyes. "Come on, Chester, you're smarter than that. Do you really think a lovely young woman like—"

"Esther."

"—like Esther would want a guy who doesn't know his way around the block, do you? If you can't knock her socks off with a mind-blowing kiss, you're as good as finished."

Chester had no idea his situation was that dire. "How do I do it? Do you know? Do you know how to give a mind-blowing kiss? You've got to teach me!"

Jahn's greasy smile widened further. "Relax, Chester, you're in good hands. If there's one thing I know it's how to kiss the ladies. Start by closing your eyes. No girl wants you staring straight into her eyeballs when your face is pressed up against hers."

Chester closed his eyes.

"Now open your mouth slightly. Trust me, this is how it works."

Chester did as he said. With his eyes closed and lips pursed, Chester imagined leaning in seductively as his lady love—

Jahn's lips mashed up against Chester's, Jahn jabbing his tongue around the inside of his mouth like a starving man desperately trying to lap up the last morsel of food. Chester spit out the invading tongue and stepped back.

"My God, what have you done?" Chester said.

Jahn's eyes wandered away from Chester, focusing up somewhere near the stockroom's ceiling. "Was that enough? Did that work?"

"What is the meaning of this?"

Jahn smiled. "Good, how long will it take?"

"Who do you think you're talking to?"

Jahn's eyes returned to Chester. He was grinning and staring at him expectantly.

"What do you—"

Hello? Testing, testing, one, two, three.

"Where in the—? Who's—"

You do hear us, don't you, Chester?

Erma found a half dozen boxes of My Miniature Pony

Cereal Bars on the overstock food aisle, from a cartoon that hadn't been on the air since 2001. And that's probably the last time anyone had cleaned back there. She wiped off a fuzzy gray layer of dust, keeping her mouth covered with her Harley Davidson T-shirt so she didn't breathe in anything that might kill her. She had first-hand experience with that. Her first husband died from black lung. Her second husband died from asbestos poisoning. Her third husband was still alive; she just wished the rotten bastard was dead.

When the dust settled and the air was clear, Erma lit a cigarette and sat on a case of Healthfast Double-Fudge Caramel Crunch Slim Bars. It was nearly four in the morning and she hadn't been up this late since her mid-forties, before she gave up crystal meth. Those were some wild times, hanging with the Lucifer's Landlords MC, partying for days at a time. She even did a porno once for drug money. She heard it was called "Queefer Madness" but she never saw it and didn't want to. She didn't want to think about those times at all. She was happy living her quiet life with her little apartment and her cat Shithead. Now, watching her soaps, *Days of Our Nights* and *The Young and the Fidgety* was her only vice. That and the cigarettes. And the whiskey.

Erma took another drag on her unfiltered Camel and saw Jahn and Chester standing at the end of the aisle, sweating and grinning at her.

"Jesus Cornelius Christ," she said, "you two haven't said a word yet and you're already bugging me."

"How's it goin'?" Jahn said. He made a kissy snarl, probably thinking he looked sexy.

Erma took a drag of her cigarette and blew a stream of smoke at them.

"You know, Erma, my friend Chester here has never kissed a girl before. What do you say you show him how it's done? I'm sure kissing a sweet young thing like yourself would be the highlight of his life."

Chester nodded, grinning dumbly.

"You know what would be the highlight of my life?" Erma said. "You two creeps leaving me alone."

"I guess I'll have to pull out the big guns," Jahn said. "You do my main man this little favor and you can have yourself a big slice of Jahnny Cake." He ran his hand over his chest, leering at her with droopy eyes.

Erma sashayed slowly over to the boys, swinging her hips, returning Jahn's grotesque seductive look with one of her own. She stopped in front of him, took a drag of her cigarette and stabbed him on the tip of the nose with the hot end.

"Ow!" Jahn screamed. "That really hurt!"

"Get out of here, creeps, I've got work to do."

Jahn scurried back to the other end of the stockroom, Chester shuffling along behind. The tip of his nose was burning and the hole in his head was raw and throbbing. He was also starting to see rotten patches and loose skin on his arms.

You're going to have to try again.

"Oh, God, not you again," Jahn said. "There's no way she's going to kiss us."

Then you're just going to have to try something else.

"I don't know what to do. Chester, are you hearing this?"

"Are you referring to our intracranial narrator? We were just discussing how much Erma looks like musician Tom Petty, only older and a woman."

Your friend hears his own voice unless you're physically touching. Why don't you hold his hand so your voices are in sync?

"Oh, come on. I'm not going to—"

Jahn doubled over as an electric jolt of pain shot through him.

"Okay, fine," he said and slapped his hand into Chester's chubby, sweaty, small-fingered mitt.

Can you both hear us?

"Yeah."

"Yes."

Fine. Now you'll have to try again to get us into your colleague. If we can't enter through her saliva, you'll have to use one of her other bodily fluids.

"If she won't kiss us, she definitely won't bone us," Jahn said.

If you were to bite her, we could enter through the blood stream.

"Bite her?" Chester said. "She'll kill us!"

"We're going to die anyway."

"What?"

We haven't told him yet.

"Hey, I heard that!"

Yes, sorry, Chester, but I'm afraid we are a fatal condition. Your body will start to decay soon.

"Mine already is," Jahn said. He pushed at an ash-colored patch on his forearm. The dead skin peeled off like a sunburn, revealing the rotten gray flesh beneath. "Oh, God. Let's just get this over with."

"I'm sorry, but I'm rather in shock right now! I've just learned of my own imminent mortality."

"I'm finding it better not to think about it," Jahn said, dragging slack-jawed Chester by his hand.

They returned to the aisle where Erma was swatting boxes lazily with her duster. She looked up at Jahn and Chester holding hands and smiled. "Well, aren't we cute."

"We want to tell you a secret," Jahn said.

Erma raised her hands. "Hey, don't ask, don't tell. That's my policy."

"I assure you," Chester said, "it's an urgent matter."

They walked hand in hand toward her. When they were close, Jahn leaned in, Erma's expression of disgust growing as he closed in. When his lips were right next to her ear, he said, "Okay, the secret is..." and bit down hard on her cheek, getting a mouthful of leathery, fuzzy skin between his teeth.

"Ah!" Erma screeched. "You stupid cocksnuggling shit-biscuits!"

She twisted to the side, Jahn spinning around her, his

teeth gripping her cheek-meat but not breaking the skin. The two of them stumbled down the aisle, slamming into the second-floor railing, nearly tumbling over the side. Jahn opened his jaw, freeing Erma's face. He looked over the edge to the concrete floor twelve feet below. "Man," he said, "that was close."

Erma lunged at him, hitting him in the chest, sending him backward over the railing, the world upended as he somersaulted backward through space, slamming awkwardly to a crunching stop.

"Don't you ever touch me, you limpdicked son of a fucktard," Erma called down at his crumpled body.

Jahn was scared to move, not sure if all his bones were broken. Slowly, he opened his eyes and saw that he'd landed on a stack of Scarlet Breeze sanitary napkins boxes. He pushed himself up. Nothing seemed to be broken, but he was sore and his skin was torn and ragged.

There was a high-pitched scream on the second floor. It sounded like a young girl.

"Stop, I implore you!" It was Chester.

Jahn ran back up the stairs, hearing Chester's terrified wailing punctuated by meaty thumps. At the top of the stairs he saw Chester on his back, Erma straddling him, pounding his face with her fists. His nose was covered in blood. He sneezed, spraying blood and mucus in Erma's face and into her mouth.

Erma got off of Chester and started toward Jahn, then stopped. She looked around, confused. "Yeah, I hear you," she said. "Who is that?"

Well done, Jahn. It looks like we have her. Now go hold her hand so we can plan our next move.

Dirk was in the manager's office, chewing the eraser off his pencil, making out the schedules for next week. He'd given up on the stockroom. That stockroom could kiss his hairy sack. It was like someone was playing some dumb-ass joke and he was the butt of it. *But Dirk Kruppie is nobody's butt!*

He'd found Viking Horn X-tra Girth Condoms in the toy and candy section. There were cases of Nickelodeon's Barf Brothers Chunky Chocolate Puke pudding cups in the Valuables Room. There were a dozen freezer-burned boxes of Jimmy Boy's Chicken Sausage Ice Cream Pops in the walk-in. Why? Nobody ate that shit! It's fucking disgusting!

So he gave up. He wasn't going to get that store manager job, just like he wasn't going to be a guitar consultant for Mötley Crüe or stunt double for Stone Cold Steve Austin or tiger trainer for Animal Ice Capades or any of his other dreams that had died over the years.

There was a pounding on the door. Erma's craggy face was looking in through the little window. "Let me in."

"No," Dirk said and went back to figuring out who could fill in while the Cosmetics girl was out with an anal fissure.

"Come on, it's important."

"Leave me alone. Chantelle's butt injury is killing me."

"What?"

"Never mind. Just leave me alone and get back to the stockroom. Crastfinger'll be here any time now."

There was frantic whispering on the other side of the door. Jahn said, "Just go on, say it."

"Hey Dirk," Erma said, sounding exasperated. "Do you want to make out? I think you're macho and hot and I really want to make out with you."

"No!" Dirk yelled. Damn, what's gotten into that girl? "As the supervising manager on duty I think your sexual advances are hella inappropriate. But that was pretty awesome what you said about me being macho and hot, so thank you for that. Now get back to work."

More frantic whispering. "But you have to come quick. Chester, uh, cut off his finger."

Dirk shook his head. "Before or after you wanted to make out with me?"

"Oh, I don't know. I just forgot for a second. Would you come out here already?"

Dirk threw his pencil down and opened the door. "Man, I'm not an assistant manager, I'm a babysit—"

Erma, Jahn and Chester lunged at him, all three waggling their tongues at his face. Erma and Jahn mashed their wet, pink organs against Dirk's sputtering lips. Chester grabbed Dirk's arm and bit down.

Dirk pushed Erma and Jahn away and threw a side thrust kick at Chester's solar plexus that launched him into the file cabinets. Chester slid to the floor, grabbing his chest and wheezing.

Dirk stepped back into a tiger stance, his fists balled. "What the hell has gotten into you? I don't care how macho and hot you think I am, you do *not* lay your hands on my person without my expressed consent. Hella, *hella* inappropriate. What was the first rule of the 'Sexual Harassment and You' workshop? 'Do not attempt to rape your fellow employees.' First goddamn rule."

"No one thinks you're hot," Erma said.

As Dirk looked at the three of them, he saw that they weren't looking so hot themselves. Their skin was covered with dark, rotten patches like old bruised bananas, and it was sagging. Erma's skin was always sagging, but now it looked like she was wearing an Erma suit that was a size too large.

Jahn looked the worst of the bunch, like chunks of him had sloughed off. "We had to attack you," he said. "We have little aliens inside us making us—" Jahn dropped to the ground, screaming and writhing in pain.

Erma dropped a second later, curled into the fetal position. "You cockslobbering sons of shitsniffing alien turdmunchers! I'll kill every one of you snotgobbling knobticklers!"

Chester was already on the ground, but now he was twisting in agony. "Why! Why, Lord! Why hast thou forsaken me!"

Whatever pain was tormenting them seemed to come to a sudden stop. They sat panting for a second, then stood.

"Uh, hello!" Dirk said. "Is one of you going to explain

what the hell you think you're doing? Y'all are acting like a bunch of paste-eating morons."

"You say one more word," Erma said to Jahn, "I'll cut your nuts off."

Jahn's droopy, blotchy face looked defeated. He looked like he was about to start crying, then straightened. A clear, calm look came over his face. He looked jerkily to the left and to the right. He raised one arm and let it drop, then the other. "Testing, testing, one, two, three," he said. "We have control of the Jahn unit. I repeat, we have control of the Jahn unit."

Erma and Chester both stiffened. "Testing, testing, one, two, three," they both said, overlapping each other. "All occupied units are under our control."

"Dirk," Jahn said, "your time is up. I suggest you submit. It will be best for all of us."

"All right, Jahn," Dirk said, "you're fired. You're fired for being a goddamn weirdo. Erma, Chester, all you freaks, get the hell out of my store. And I mean now. Do not test me. I will shake your foundation."

"I'm afraid that's not possible," Jahn said. "We have a mission to complete and you are the next phase of our plan. Do not bother to resist. You are no longer dealing with your former colleagues. You are dealing with an intergalactic, aeonian intelligence."

"Oh yeah," Dirk said. "Well, you're dealing with a motherfucking blackbelt. Bring it on, douchebag."

"Suit yourself," Jahn said. "But I warn you: you will be

crushed. We are not three. We are infinite."

Jahn, Erma and Chester jerked and flopped toward Dirk like all their limbs had fallen asleep, awkwardly flapping their rubbery arms at him.

Dirk spun into action. Roundhouse kick! Roundhouse kick! Roundhouse kick! He knocked all three back out of the office and into the hallway before shutting and locking the office door. He was out of breath, sweat making his blond hair stick to his forehead. He spoke through the door's little window. "I'm sorry," pant, "that I had to unleash," pant, "the full force of my," pant, "taekwondo training on that ass," pant, "but you three are starting," pant, "to freak me out."

Dirk flopped into the manager's chair. "Bouncing Baby Jesus," he said. He needed to catch his breath and figure out what was going on. But he decided not to figure anything out and just rest for a while. He didn't even think about Mr. Crastfinger until he heard everyone running after him.

Crastfinger checked his watch. It was precisely five a.m. and no one was at the front of the store to let him in. He generously waited sixty seconds more, then put a red check on his Store Inspection Report. The stock form didn't have a box for "Timely greeting of Inspector," but Crastfinger had added the field. He had added a number of fields because the form was insufficient. He had added checkboxes for "Product labels facing outward," "Restrooms have pleasant odor," "Robust esprit de corps," and many more. And now the first box at the very top of the page had an ugly red mark.

This gave Crastfinger a great deal of pleasure. He had to savor these little victories over the slackers and crumb-bums of the world. His wife may be a shrieking two-ton harpy and his son may be a bespectacled poet with the complexion of a tall glass of skim milk but, by God, Senior Regional Manager Horace Crastfinger had satisfaction in his life! The satisfaction of making dead certain the incompetents and layabouts felt the crushing weight of his judgment and the sting of his mighty red pen.

Crastfinger and his pen went to the stockroom where the most egregious violations would certainly be found. As he walked up aisle one, the motley crew of low-wage laborers finally showed themselves. And it wasn't a pretty sight. They looked like melting wax statues.

"Don't move!" said a drooping, dreadlocked teenager. "I'm going to put my saliva in you."

"You're what?" Crastfinger said. "You're going to put your what in my what?"

"My saliva. I'm going to put it into your body now."

"The hell you are!" Crastfinger yelled, shaking his red pen at them.

"You are in no position to refuse," the sagging boy said. "You're dealing with a superior intelligence. Prepare to submit!"

The three came stumbling after Crastfinger, wobbling and stiff-legged like Frankenstein's monster's alcoholic cousins.

Crastfinger was dumbstruck, unsure how seriously he should take these stumbling, floppy-fleshed freaks. But then a round, squishy boy pulled a boxcutter from his polyester vest as if brandishing a sword.

Crastfinger dashed into the stockroom. He looked around and saw the Valuables Room where they kept anything worth more than twenty dollars. It was just a small corner of the stockroom partitioned off with plywood and chicken wire, but it had a lock.

The freaks burst through the swinging doors, stomping into the stockroom like they didn't have knees.

Crastfinger scrambled through his ring of keys, found the right one and jammed it into the padlock.

The freaks lumbered toward him. "Stop delaying the inevitable," the dreadlocked boy said. "I command you to open your mouth. Prepare to receive my juices."

Crastfinger opened the lock, slipped into the room and locked it from the inside.

The freaks threw themselves at the door and pounded at the chicken wire.

Crastfinger searched the room for something he could use as a weapon. Uncle Sam's Freedom Fryers, iBall SoundOrb bluetooth speakers, DeezNutz Hip-Hop Headgear noise canceling headphones. Nothing!

The round boy chopped at the plywood with his boxcutter. The other boy grabbed the chicken wire and yanked, his dreadlocks flying forward and back as he pulled, until something ripped at the back of his head and his entire scalp slid forward, taking his face with it, revealing the red, skeletal visage beneath.

The old woman found a corner of the chicken wire wall and started peeling.

"It's only a matter of time now," the faceless boy said, his hair hanging like a knotted beard across his chest. "It's only a matter of time."

Dirk was spacing out when he heard his employees scramble around the corner. He looked at the clock; it was precisely five a.m. That meant Crastfinger was there, and he was about to have an ugly old woman stick her tongue in his mouth. That couldn't happen. No one deserved that.

Dirk slipped out of the office and saw the employees chase Crastfinger into the stockroom. And that seemed about right. He knew that one way or another tonight was going to come down to the stockroom. Whether it was the inspector telling him he did a shitty job of keeping it clean, or a final badass Steven Seagal-style showdown with some alien buttholes, Dirk knew it was all about the stockroom.

He pushed the door open a crack and saw the employees had Crastfinger trapped in the Valuables Room like an old, bald rat. Dirk sneaked up the stairs to the stockroom's second floor. He crept to the far north corner and positioned himself right above them. He could drop straight onto one of their backs, but it was a good dozen feet. He needed something to slow his fall. There was a dusty gray blanket covering a pallet of Mama Snooki's Old World Italiano canned lasagna. He tied one end of the blanket around his neck. He could grab the other end when he jumped to create a parachute effect.

Dirk spotted the back-support belt he left up there earlier. That could come in handy. As he strapped it on, an idea struck him like a bolt of lightning straight from Thor's long, swinging hammer.

Dirk turned the back-support belt around so the wide section was in the front. It looked just like a WWE championship belt. And the blanket hanging from his neck was a cape. It brought him back to being a scrawny eight-year-old kid watching his favorite wrestler—The Flying Caucasian— jump off the top turnbuckle to smash the face of his nemesis Sheik Abu al-Insani with a Flying Elbow Drop. But now, as if his entire life had been leading up to this moment, it was Dirk Kruppie who was about to strike a blow against the forces of evil. It was time to be a motherfucking hero.

Dirk grabbed the bottom corners of the cape and yelled, "Big Kahuna!"

The cape did nothing to slow his fall. He dropped full-speed and landed on Jahn, who exploded like a bag of pudding, spraying chunky red liquid in every direction. For a moment no one moved, the only sound a wet plopping as chunks of Jahn dripped off the walls and stacked boxes.

Erma grabbed an unidentifiable organ, and said to Chester, "Get these into its mouth. Overwhelm him with human essence!" The two chucked squishy handfuls at Dirk, hunks of meat flapping against his upper torso as he struggled to his feet, every muscle feeling like he'd been doing power squats with a dump truck.

Erma chucked a lung at Dirk's face. He swatted it away and picked her up by her legs, leaping into the air while throwing his own legs around her head. He came down in a textbook piledriver, popping her noggin like a swatted mosquito.

That left Chester—and his boxcutter. If it even nicked him, those alien creepy-crawlies would get in his blood and make him a saggy douchebag. There was no time for fancy ass-kicking. He had to keep it real. Real as steel.

Chester raised his boxcutter.

Dirk balled his fist and pulled back.

Chester charged him, slashing with the cutter.

Dirk blocked with his left and swung his right with such magnificent force it knocked Chester's head clean off his neck and sent it splattering against the wall behind him as his spurting body dropped to the wet floor.

Crastfinger was curled up in the corner, pressed up against a case of J. Cousteau cologne.

"It's okay," Dirk said. "The alien threat has been neutralized."

Crastfinger stood, and with shaky hands, he unlocked theValuables Room door. "Are you sure it's safe?"

"That's affirmative."

Crastfinger stiffened his spine and pulled back his shoulders. "Sir, what you have done here today…" His chin quivered. "I'll just say that you, my friend, will be rewarded for your efforts."

Dirk sniffed and nodded. "Hell yeah."

Spendthrift's fluorescent lights buzzed on for the first time in three days. The stockroom had been sanitized, and to show his appreciation for Dirk's efforts, Crastfinger hired a full crew out of the corporate budget to come in the previous night and organize the stock. He'd also approved Dirk's plan for this morning's events.

All of the store's surviving employees were in attendance. Even Chantelle, despite her butt injury. Dirk positioned them along both sides of the Hardware and Garden Supplies aisle. Crastfinger stood at the far end and Dirk was at the other. Dirk placed the *Karate Kid II* soundtrack cassette in his boombox and pressed Play. When Peter Cetera's manly voice came in, Dirk began to march up the aisle.

'I am a man who will fight for your honor,

I'll be the hero you're dreaming of.'

Dirk walked proudly down the aisle past his admiring colleagues, chin held high, awesome blond hair feathered and flowing. When he reached Crastfinger, he removed his orange polyester vest, folded it once and folded it again.

'Just like a knight in shining armor,

from a long time ago.

Just in time I will save the day,

take you to my castle far away.'

Dirk knelt and held the vest aloft.

Crastfinger took the vest and set it on the Craig T. Nelson Celebrity Signature Series Patio Table. He then picked up the black manager's vest and placed it on Dirk's upturned palms.

"With this vest," Crastfinger said, "I pronounce you Store Manager for Spendthrift Drug and Discount, East Billingham. May you wear it with pride and manage with honor."

The employees gave Dirk a rousing ovation as he rose and donned the vest. It looked good on him. It looked right. "Thank you," Dirk said. "Thank you all. We lost some good people the other night, but I swear they will not have died in vain. As your manager, I will—"

The stockroom door burst open, and the crew who'd been organizing the stock stumbled out, skin drooping.

"Testing."

"Testing, testing, one, two."

"One, two, three."

"Testing."

"Testing, one, two."

"Testing, testing."

"One, two, three."

The employees screamed. Crastfinger clutched his chest. It was pandemonium.

But Dirk didn't panic. He uncoiled two extension cords. "Everyone behind me." He gave the ends to Crastfinger. "Find an outlet."

As a dozen alien monstrosities shambled toward him, Dirk attached the extension cords to two electric chainsaws.

"Okay, Crastfinger, plug 'em in."

Crastfinger did as he was told.

The alien crew raised their boxcutters, tongues wagging.

"Don't worry, Crastfinger," Dirk said. "You made me a manager." He revved the chainsaws. "Now I'm gonna manage this bitch."

Dying Art

C L Raven

I didn't consider myself to be a serial killer; I was a craftsman.

"Don't struggle. I don't want to hurt you."

The man stared at me, his eyes wide, his lips pulled back against the gag, creating a macabre grin the Joker would covet. I covered his face with a pillow so I wouldn't have his death mask haunting me whenever I closed my eyes. The last thing I needed was a conscience keeping me awake. The screaming baby next door already had that role.

While there were quicker ways to kill someone, suffocation didn't damage bones or skin. Yes, they suffered for longer, but sacrifices had to be made for the perfect materials. I was an artist, not a doctor. If I cared about their suffering, I wouldn't kill them. I'd once ruined two perfectly good ribs because I'd stabbed someone in the heart. That mistake left me short for a fruit bowl so someone else had to die to compensate. It was very inconvenient. I hated dashing out for supplies when I was in the middle of a project.

Besides, it wasn't about killing. I didn't get some bizarre sexual thrill from it, I wasn't fulfilling a violent fantasy, and I wasn't on a mission from God. It didn't silence the demons —I didn't have any. There would be no documentary reveling in my depravity. No psychologists pondering if my normal upbringing was responsible and whether attending a dolls' house convention aged five planted the seeds in my mind. I needed what the body contained and, to do that, I had to take lives. Like cutting down a tree to make books.

The man fought, as desperate to cling to his life as I was to take it. I hated when they struggled. My job was tiring and caused a lot of back ache, so I disliked having to fight for my materials. A lumberjack never had to wrestle a tree into submission.

His body bucked and he landed hard on the edge of the bed. *Snap.*

"You've ruined my project! Now I'm going to have to find another supplier or it will be late. We all have to die. I don't see why you're fighting it. At least you'll live on. Think of it as reincarnation. It's better than being in a coffin or an urn in the ground. Families will pass your bones down with the inheritance. More people will see the chair than your grave."

I used to explain it wasn't personal, it was business, but people get irrational when you're trying to kill them. I'd even shown one woman the beautiful baroque chairs she was contributing to, but that made her panic more. Maybe she preferred art deco.

I pressed harder on the pillow and the man eventually stopped struggling. I threw the pillow aside and examined his broken arm. I couldn't use that. It broke right in the middle. I flung his arm down. His arms were the exact size I needed, and his athletic frame hinted at excellent bone density. God knows where I'd find another supplier on such short notice. I couldn't exactly phone a warehouse and order more stock.

I dragged him into my workshop and set him down in the preparation corner, which resembled a wet room. I donned my work suit and laid out my tools. This wasn't my favourite part of the job—ruptured organs have a foul stench no amount of odour neutraliser can remove—but it was like unwrapping a very messy Christmas present to see what gifts Father Christmas had brought.

I swiftly undressed the man, then carefully flayed him. Once I'd removed his skin, I took it into another part of my workshop, where I laid it on the cold floor and covered it in salt. Now for the messy part. The man's body was a grotesque husk of blood, bone and ligaments. Barely human. His eyes stared at me in horror, stark white against his bloody face.

"Don't look at me like that. Your death would've been easier if you hadn't struggled. You only have yourself to blame."

I carried several tubs to the body and removed the organs. Some went in a box to be disposed of later— intestines might look like sausages but they weren't really a delicacy and I had yet to find a use for the genitals. The stomach wasn't worth keeping either, unless I started force-feeding my suppliers to make my own foie gras. But I was a carpenter, not a chef. Edible parts went in separate Tupperware boxes. The neighbourhood barbeque was next week and my artisan burgers were firm favourites. I placed the tubs in my chest freezer and then scraped muscles, ligaments and tendons off the bones, being careful not to nick them, before I boiled the final remnants off.

I frowned at the broken arm bone. Maybe I could use it as inlay. Throwing it out seemed such a waste. I cleaned the bones, then arranged them into separate boxes in my work cabinet. I had plenty of metatarsals and phalanges, but never enough femurs. What I needed were suppliers with arms and legs but no hands or feet to balance out my stock supplies. A human octopus would be ideal.

Now came my least favourite part—washing the preparation room. I suppose everyone has parts of their job they hate. At least I wasn't working in retail, dealing with irate customers. But where was the creativity in scrubbing a room? Nobody won awards for how well they handled a mop. But it was better to clean up before the blood had a chance to stain. Getting dried blood out of grouting was a nightmare, and I couldn't exactly hire someone to do it for me. People took a dim view of being an accessory to murder, even if it paid well.

I laid the bones out on my workbench and studied my sketches. The chair back was a ladder design but with a spine down the centre and ribs forming the ladder. My client was building a horror house attraction and wanted furniture to look as though it was made of human bones. I think she'd like what was I was creating. It was all about aesthetics. Also on her list were a table, a skull lamp with a spine forming the stand, a wind chime with a skull on the top and arm bones hanging from it, and a bone chandelier like the one in the Sedlec Ossuary near Prague. She also wanted a throne made from skulls. I finally had a use for my surplus skulls. They were cluttering up the place and making it look like a bizarre museum.

I glued the spine together. Fortunately, my supplier didn't show signs of osteoporosis. The last thing anyone wanted was a chair that collapsed under them because the supplier hadn't drunk enough milk.

While the spine glue hardened, I worked on the chair frame. This was where the larger bones were used, but I never had enough. Yes, I could use animal bones as substitutes but that would make my business tagline false advertising: 'made with humans, not machines.' People liked buying bespoke handmade furniture. But tell them their new chair was made from something that talked instead of mooed and suddenly they got righteous about living things. The truth was, I loved animals. People could be shitty. Kill a harmless cow or some wanker who tried to sideswipe me off the motorway? I could buy bones from the butcher's, but that didn't make good business sense when I could get my own free materials.

I also loved creating unique furniture. Making things from animals was unoriginal. Plus, the world was running out of space to bury the dead; I was merely contributing to the solution. Turning your loved ones' remains into something decorative was all the rage now. Was a diamond made from ashes really any better than a chair? People complained about cheap, mass-produced flat pack, bemoaning, 'They don't make them like they used to.' I was keeping traditional skills alive.

As the frame glue dried, I fetched previously tanned skin and cut it to size, stretching it over the chair cushion and stapling it in place. This one I'd dyed a red wine colour. It fitted with the horror house's period look. I covered three more cushions with the red leather then returned to making the chair frames.

When I had four frames setting, I turned my attention to another part of my business—making dolls' house furniture. This was where the metatarsals and phalanges came in useful. Not all of the dolls' house furniture was made from bone; however, my most popular item was tiny bone china crockery. Every detail hand painted.

Talent like mine couldn't be bought in stores.

But now, I needed more materials.

I parked and waited. Among the other taxis, mine wouldn't be noticed. The taxi plate looked genuine and honestly, who even checked? Some people I picked up could barely manage to open the door; they definitely weren't investigating the legitimacy of my plate.

A man stumbled toward the taxis. Perfect. Most drivers wanted groups. More people, bigger fares. I wanted lone passengers. People who might not be reported missing immediately. Taxi driving was a means to get supplies rather than a dedicated career—I already had one of those. But it was nice to get out of my workshop every now and again. I stepped out of the taxi so the man would notice me. He staggered toward me and I opened the back door, closing it when he slid in. The child locks would ensure he couldn't escape. Car manufacturers' concern for child safety made kidnapping someone so much easier. He gave me his address and I put it into SatNav but it was just a ruse.

He wasn't going home.

I reversed out of the space, a hundred witnesses oblivious to this man's kidnap and subsequent murder. Maybe some of these people would even buy the furniture and accessories I made from his bones. Running a successful business from home was nearly impossible in today's economy but somehow, I was succeeding. This man would further that success. To think, he probably thought his night would end with his head down a toilet.

His open mouth pressed against the plastic bag, his wide bloodshot eyes pleading with me to stop. I regretted using a clear bag, but it was the only one I had. I didn't want to go to the newsagents for a white one. Muffled cries escaped him, his hands flailing uselessly, occasionally slapping me but never getting a grip. I pulled harder on the bag, twisting it around his neck so he couldn't fight his way free. He didn't think to puncture a hole near his mouth. They never do. They fight hard, not smart. Humans like to think they're the hunters but really, they're each other's prey.

Finally, he slumped, defeated. I kept the bag on until I was sure he was dead. I'd fallen for that trick before. When I was satisfied he wasn't faking death, I removed the bag and carried him down to my workshop. At least this one hadn't broken any bones. I laid him out and removed his clothes. I'd donate them to charity after a few months had passed. I was in desperate need of good karma.

Music played while I worked. It relaxed me and stopped neighbours complaining about any noise. The last thing I wanted was to be the subject of a Neighbourhood Watch meeting, or, heaven forbid, its newsletter.

I picked up my razor and shaved him. Hairy men were the worst. Nobody wanted furry furniture, so they just made extra work for me. Women's smoother skin took less preparation time and resulted in lovely soft leather, but for this commission, I needed bigger bones. Plus I didn't want to be dubbed 'the next Ed Gein'. I didn't have mother issues. I'd considered using the salvaged breast implants as padding in my furniture, but the serial numbers would trace back to the victims, so I had a drawer full of silicone boobs, like a weird stress ball collection. It surprised me how many women had fake breasts. I thought it was exclusive to models and strippers, but even your average Mandy who worked at the local supermarket was sporting them. The nice thing about women was I could cut off their hair and donate it to a 'wigs for kids' charity. I liked giving back to the community.

When I reached the hand, I stopped.

"Six fingers? I don't need more phalanges and you have to go all Anne Boleyn on me. Couldn't you have had an extra leg?"

I sighed and continued shaving him. First he was hairy, now this. Luckily he didn't break a bone or I might have made him suffer for his selfishness. Who was I kidding? I was no Jack the Ripper. I skinned him, then stripped him to his skeleton. At least his bones were in good condition. I measured his humerus against the chair. Too long. I'd have to cut it. That would add time to the project. My client could afford it.

The music ended, so I put the news on while I fetched leather for the dolls' house. I wanted updates to see if anyone had reported my suppliers missing. A press conference came on. I didn't pay attention until the words 'missing man' were spoken. I looked up and saw an earlier victim's photo on screen. His mother sobbed about how she and his father wanted him home safely. I glanced at the leather I held. It was too late for a safe return. I rarely remember which part belonged to which victim, but he'd had numerous tattoos, so I'd had to discard most of his skin.

I used his skin to cover the dolls' house armchairs. They were wingback chairs that were fiddly to make but turned out perfectly. I'd dyed the leather a beautiful burnt umber. Unfortunately, I didn't have a buyer but I would be exhibiting them in a dolls' house convention in two weeks. I stabbed my finger with the sewing needle more than I stabbed the leather, but it was more precise than a sewing machine. I covered a settee with the skin from his feet. I hated to waste any part. It was a shame I could never do anything with eyes, but they weren't exactly decorative and had a nasty habit of decomposing. Eyeball juice ruined a good design.

I turned my attention to a bedside cabinet while the cramp in my fingers eased. It was a simple three-drawer mahogany one in a French style, but the client wanted ivory inlay. I don't believe elephants and rhinos should die for bedroom furniture. Plus, the ban on ivory products made it illegal. I persuaded him that bone was equally as beautiful and wouldn't endanger a species. After all, humans weren't at risk of going extinct. They were what environmentalists call a 'renewable resource'.

I fetched a bag of bone chips from the drawer and shaved bits off until they were the correct shape. The client wanted an irregular pattern, which made life easier. Indian-style inlay was extremely fiddly. When I had all the pieces, I laid them out on the top of the cabinet and drew around them. I spent hours carving out niches for the bone to sit in. This was the trickiest part of the job. Too large and the bone piece wouldn't fit. I sanded the wood I'd carved out to make dust and mixed it with epoxy so it would be the same colour as the cabinet. I poured generous amounts of glue into the holes, then carefully put the bone pieces in. I'd have to wait for it to dry before sanding the inlay flat.

I smiled as I ran my hand along the top of the cabinet. This really was a dying art.

Rows of dolls' houses filled the convention centre. They ranged from simple bungalows to Victorian townhouses. Some were replicas of famous horror houses from movies or TV: *The Addams Family, Amityville Horror, Bates Motel, American Horror Story: Murder House.* One was an exact replica of the Winchester Mystery House. I was secretly in awe of that one and wished I'd done it, but it would have taken months to make and I didn't have the time. Some traders only sold empty houses, some only sold furniture, some only sold dolls. There was even one selling flat pack houses. I found the dolls creepy. Miniature people with stiff limbs and dead eyes. It was like they were selling corpses masquerading as the living.

I'd made a tiny bone inlay cabinet which took me longer than the life-sized version had, and I placed it at the front of the table. I scrutinised the other tables. Whilst it was clear lots of hard work went into each piece, they weren't made with the blood, sweat and tears that mine were.

A little girl ran up to my table. "Mummy, I want this." She picked up a four-poster bed.

Some bone pieces were worked into intricate designs, with a random scattering of jewels that I'd taken from some suppliers' jewellery. I'd cut lace off my supplier's skirt to make the curtains and satin from her underwear to make the bedding.

"It's too expensive to be played with," her mum replied. "We'll find cheaper furniture for your dolls' house."

"It's all handmade." I smiled at them. "And built to last. Her grandchildren will be playing with it."

The mum examined the furniture, nostalgia making her smile. "My nan had a stool like this." She picked up a small footstool with bowed legs and an orange leather cushion, finished with studs.

"So did mine, that's why I made it. I don't just make furniture, I make memories." If that was any cheesier, a lactose intolerant person would be sick. But it always worked.

She bought the stool. I wrapped it and put it in a box with my business card. A couple of hours passed with a few small sales. A woman bought my set of tiny bone china plates with the fern leaf pattern. People were admiring my wares but not buying. Price was usually the deciding factor. I worked all hours to make these; I couldn't afford to give them away. I had to eat and pay bills. Plus, it would do my suppliers a disservice. Their lives were worth more than a fifty per cent discount.

During a lull in the convention, I took the opportunity to make more pieces. If people saw me working, it might convince them to buy. I made bone walking sticks from phalanges, carefully carving the heads to a perfect curved finish. I also made miniature wind chimes, hanging them on an earring stand while they dried.

A man stopped by my table. "Your work is the best I've seen." I couldn't argue with that. "I'm in the process of commissioning a dolls' house — an exact replica of my house that I can display. I was wondering if you would be interested in making the furniture."

"Absolutely. If you send me photos of everything you want, I can give you a price per item or an overall estimate." I handed him a business card. "I specialise in period or unusual pieces."

"I live in Borwood House. You are welcome to come and take your own photos."

I'd driven past it once. It was a huge Georgian mansion that occasionally had open days to help pay towards restoration and maintenance. I started picturing the style of furniture and the number of rooms. This would be a big project.

"Let me know when is convenient for you."

The man handed me his business card and left. Borwood House. No doubt the dolls' house would be displayed at an open day. Thousands of people would see my work. I was going to need a lot more supplies. The convention dragged now that I was excited about a new project. I watched people walking past, calculating how many pieces of furniture I could make from them.

An hour passed without a sale. As I started to despair, a middle-aged couple came over. They looked familiar. They quietly admired my furniture, then the man picked up one of the wingback armchairs.

"These would finish off the dolls' mansion perfectly." He turned it over, examining it closely. "Your work is exquisite."

"I carefully source my materials. A single piece can take

me hours, but it's worth it."

"We'll take the two armchairs and the settee. And also the side table."

I wrapped them up. As I was handing over the furniture, I realised where I recognised the couple from: the press conference about the missing man. Well, they partly got their wish. Their son would be going home with them. They'd bought the furniture covered in his skin.

Tea Time

William West

Merrill craned her neck to get a better look at Grace snoring on the ceiling. She considered screaming, but thought it wouldn't do to panic on an empty stomach. Anyway, the tea needed brewing.

A quarter hour later, Merrill sat down on the divan behind the coffee table spread with Grace's good china, triangle-cut cucumber sandwiches, pastel iced petit fours, and a teapot with wisps of vapor coming out the spout. Grace had hardly shifted from her gravity-defying slumber.

Merrill briefly reconsidered the panic option, but the tea would probably get cold, and *that* would be cause for hysterics. She felt ambivalent about waking her sister up, but whatever witchcraft this was, she'd be damned if she was going to have tea alone.

"Grace."

Nothing.

"Grace!"

The ceiling-bound woman stirred, and a subtle tremor rattled the teacups.

"Fine," said Merrill, "I'll have tea without you."

Grace's eyes opened and looked down at Merrill, who squinted up at two glowing orbs where her sister's eyes should have been. This did not sit well. For that matter, there was very little sitting well, and the things that did sit well were about to get up and walk out.

Merrill would have none of it. "Are you coming down?"

Grace's mouth hung open and emitted a terrible booming voice, solid enough to crush poor Merrill under its weight. "You dare disturb my slumber?"

Merrill's ears weren't so good in her dotage, and the terrific impact of this otherworldly voice was lost on her. "Well?" she asked. "Am I eating this all by myself?"

"What is 'this' you speak of?" The voice cracked like thunder.

"This?" Merrill pointed at the tea service.

"Ah. It is a sacrifice. Do you beg for your soul?" Grace's mouth moved but never seemed to catch up to the words coming out.

"What? No! It's a tea. T-E-A. Tea. And, I'm not begging for jack!" In spite (or maybe because) of everything, Merrill's empty stomach was complaining, and it made her grumpy.

"I will try." Grace dropped off the ceiling and landed upright, silent like a cat.

Merrill poured tea into their cups. "Will you sit down, or are you a horse?"

Grace sat in the easy chair across the table.

"Here you are, dear." Merrill passed her sister a cup and saucer. She could pretend everything was normal so long as she didn't look at those 'eyes'.

Of course she looked, and those 'eyes' looked back. Some metaphysical switch flipped or broke or the universe picked that day to be interesting, and for a brief second she saw herself through her sister's eyes and noticed that her roots were showing and her nose was just a little crooked.

Quick as that, Merrill was back to herself—only slightly more self-conscious.

Grace took a sip of her tea. Merrill tasted the tea as it fell into her sister's mouth and burst into sensations she'd never felt before or rather never really paid attention to—heat, wet, a tannic bitterness, a subtle jolt that ran through her body. Alongside the sensuous rush ran alien thoughts, bumping and jostling to get ahead of a new experience that should have been old hat.

Merrill fell back to her own senses, her heart beating like she'd seen her first crush walk by the window. She'd felt Grace's presence in that moment, but it was smothered in something inhuman; an unsated bloodlust that wrapped her sister's mind like swaddling.

"Tea," the voice growled, its bombast gone. Grace relaxed into her chair. Her eyelids half closed, leaving two red crescents glowing under them. Her mouth tried to curl into a smile, and some tea dribbled down her chin.

Merrill hadn't moved since she looked into those eyes, but her mind was racing. She'd sharpened it over decades at the senior center, feigning bad hearing just to get the local gossip to bring back to her and Grace's teatime kvetch-sessions, then making up the dirt once her hearing started really going. That sharp-as-a-tack mind put itself to work in the background from the moment she'd found her sister on the ceiling.

"Who are you?" she blurted out.

"My name is unspeakable by your little mind. What signifies an existence in Hell? An infinite torment? The joy I will derive from it? That would be the correct name."

My first husband, thought Merrill. "Harold."

The voice spoke. It sounded to Merrill like a two-bit dictator with a cigar in one hand and a scotch in the other, lounging with his smoking jacket open and nothing underneath. "Harold. *Har*old. Har*old.* I, Harold, am the bringer of darkness from the darkness within. The ender of worlds." Grace's face screwed up into a facsimile of a smile. "I enjoyed sharing the experience of tea with you. You must be close to this—" Grace's hand lifted and waved back and forth in front of her face, "—host." Her mouth finally caught up with the words that came out of it. "I'm not used to sharing my experiences."

"Is Grace okay?"

"The host lives." Grace—rather, Harold—took another sip, and Merrill felt the warmth of the tea flow through her. "She won't for long. Neither will you." Grace's body leaned toward Merrill. "Let me give you a parting gift." Those eyes glowed like hellfire as they bored into Merrill's, and she felt her senses dragged out of her head and strung through twisting space to a burning plain filled with stampeding customer service representatives crushing one another underfoot, braying about loyalty card discounts, and waving inch-thick terms of service pamphlets. The soil turned red with the blood of service industry drones. The remnants of a great domed city of melted skyscrapers and broken spires lay before her. She looked down and found herself standing on the bones of the last reality television star—an Emmy shoved through its gaping mandible. Desert winds carried the scent of burnt coffee and microwaved fish. The smell comforted like hot chocolate by the fireplace and a dog-eared *Reader's Digest*. She wanted for all the worlds to laugh with joy.

She returned to the living room and found a contented smile washing over her face.

"Mmmm," said Harold. "You liked my handiwork."

"Horse feathers." Merrill deeply regretted the lack of hard liquor in the house.

"What you saw was my last great work." Harold proffered its empty cup. "I have no tea."

Merrill poured. Harold tipped the cup into Grace's mouth and Merrill felt the tea in her own mouth like it was the first time she'd ever tasted it. Then she felt a jolt or shiver, and she found herself more alert than she'd felt in years. *Maybe,* she thought, *this beast likes its caffeine.*

"Tea is good," said Harold.

Merrill pointed to the sandwiches. "Have you tried one of these?"

"What is one of these?"

"These are cucumber sandwiches. A favorite. You might like them."

Grace's hand took one and smashed it on her tongue.

Chunks fell into her lap. A rush of cold and creamy textures hit Merrill square in the jaw, and something stung her tongue. She almost yelped.

Harold spoke through half-chewed sandwich, "I think it bit me."

Merrill took another sandwich and peeled it open. "This is cucumber. This is cream cheese. They cool the tongue. The bite's from these little black specks. Freshly ground peppercorns. They give it a kick."

"More." Its voice was less dictator and more used car salesman.

Merrill almost hesitated. She was tasting all the things that Grace, or Harold, or whatever had taken her over, tasted. But, this kind of intensity was liable to bowl her right out of her seat. "Try these," she said. "They have chopped jalapeño mixed in the cream cheese." Might as well make life interesting—what was left of it.

Harold put a jalapeño sandwich to Grace's mouth, this time taking an actual bite. Merrill felt the tang and burn tenfold what she expected, but she didn't cry out. Grace's face went blotchy, and sweat popped up across her forehead.

"It's beautiful!" it wheezed through the heat.

Merrill spoke through her own gritted teeth. "What do you usually eat?"

Harold washed the sandwich down with the rest of its tea. "Destroying worlds takes too much time and effort for this 'eating'. But, I deeply appreciate these new sensations, so I will not flay the nerves from under your skin today."

"You're welcome?" Merrill tried very hard not to imagine what flaying nerves might entail. On the other hand, none of her great-grandchildren visited on Christmas, so they could use a little flaying.

"You could say I consume the lamentations of the damned. But, that's nothing to this tea. I want more tea."

No manners at all, Merrill thought. It was like this beast from hell was galling her on purpose. It wasn't enough to threaten to end the world. It had to whine and wheedle her out of every drop of tea she had. All that on top of taking over her beloved sister and the only fellow human being she had anything in common with on this Earth.

Like anyone with a well-developed maternal instinct nearing the end of her rope, she took corrective action. "Say the magic word."

Up to that moment, Grace's face was alternately scowling and smiling and otherwise giving off an aura of "I'm better than you." Now, it went slightly-constipated-while-swallow-ing-a-lemon, and Merrill found herself along for another inter-dimensional joyride, seeing a rush of stars and psyche-delic locales superimposed on the living room around her. Much to her relief, she was more a spectator this time—she hadn't completely recovered from the last trip.

They flitted from world to world, through ornate and foreboding booklined edifices, sifting through ancient vol-umes from countless shelves, each written in a different indecipherable tongue. Still, she caught a glimmer of their meanings. Among the thousand tomes, she witnessed the

Necronomicon's mind-twisting horror. She marveled at the ornate beauty and the awesome truth of the Principia Discordia. She recoiled from the soul shredding Funniest Joke on One Hundred and One Planes. And, she wept at the emotional purity of A Comprehensive List of Available Area Code 212 Numbers. All this took place over centuries. Yet, the trip was over in seconds.

Grace's mouth opened and uttered the unearthly, and Merrill recognized words born of evil and made to crack the firmament. Though, to be honest, they sounded a lot like Grace clearing her throat with a plunger.

"Are you trying to wake the dead?" said Merrill.

"I—" Harold's voice had lost what was left of its imposing grandeur. "I just wanted to find the magic word."

"Please."

"What?"

"The magic word is 'please' as in 'may I please have some more tea' or 'may I have some more tea, please.' I don't know what they teach you where you come from, but it's absolutely appalling, your lack of manners. I mean, do you even—"

"May I have some more tea, please?" Grace's face twisted itself up until it looked a lot like the original Harold's face when the end of the world was nigh because he was out of gin—desperate puppy dog eyes (glowing pools of the damned, yes, but still eye-like enough).

"Of course," Merrill said, and she poured a fresh cup for *this* Harold. She had to laugh, at least to herself. This great interdimensional power didn't understand everyday human existence. She bet it would think her sister was broken when poor Grace peed herself with all that tea. It was a great contradiction, and Merrill could not fathom it.

Harold took the warm cup and sipped from it and still managed to slosh some tea on Grace's face. Merrill felt that slam of hot, wet stimulation on her own face. *Why am I thinking of cigarettes?* For the first time in years, Merrill wanted to smoke.

"Harold, would you like to try a petit four?" Merrill pointed to a tidy pyramid of pastel iced cakes.

Grace's fingers closed around a pink and green cube—hard and silky, no bigger than her thumb—and dropped it on her tongue.

Merrill felt a flush of heat fly across Grace's body, and something shouted *more*. Along with it, Merrill felt a wash of euphoria, and *her* brain shouted *more*. She got dizzy from the alien mind twisting itself up in confusion from this blast of sweet.

Merrill felt like faint, dizzy, and awake all at once. *Was this what a baby felt with her first taste of candy?* Then she crashed, melting along with the cake on her sister's tongue. And choked.

Grace coughed and gagged and wheezed.

"Wash it down, you silly fool!" Merrill recovered enough to push a teacup at Grace's face. "You're not supposed to swallow the whole thing at once! How in the hell are you this high-and-mighty devil when you about kill yourself on a cake?" For the first time she was scared, not for the beast (Was it even killable? It wasn't very sympathetic at any rate.) but for Grace. To Merrill, the rest of the world could burn, but poor Grace didn't deserve any of this. It was time to put this grand nonsense to a stop.

Merrill pulled the tea service toward her while Grace finished coughing and sputtering.

"Another," Harold wheezed.

"No."

"May I have another petit four, please?"

"No."

"I said the magic word." Its voice wheedled like Aunt Mildred's when she ran out of smokes.

"No."

Grace's body leaned forward. Her hand reached out toward the little cakes.

Merrill slapped it away.

Harold drew Grace's body out of the chair, stood and scowled, and pointed a finger at Merrill. The red orbs that were once eyes spat globs of sizzling light.

Merrill braced herself against a fresh swell of emotion. Not anger. Not even pride. She found herself floating on waves of desperation spilling from this beast whose entire being focused on tea and silly morsels. This beast was broken.

And I broke it.

Harold's voice loomed like a deep and terrible maw about to swallow the room whole. "You dare touch what is mine?"

Merrill felt the very Earth bow down before the beast. But, she sat on the divan with her back straight and her hands folded neatly in her lap, and she looked the beast right in the orbs and said, "How do you make tea?"

Silence.

"How do you make cucumber sandwiches?"

Silence.

"How do you make petit fours?"

Silence.

"Sit down, Harold. I have a proposal."

Merrill craned her neck to get a better look at Grace on the ceiling. She considered waking her up, but figured Harold would be bored twiddling its thumbs if the tea wasn't ready.

A quarter hour later, Merrill sat down on the divan behind the coffee table spread with Grace's good china, triangle-cut cucumber sandwiches, pastel iced petit fours, and a teapot with wisps of vapor coming out the spout.

Grace had hardly shifted from her gravity-defying slumber.

"Harold."

Nothing.

"Harold!"

The ceiling-bound woman stirred, and a subtle tremor rattled the teacups.

"Fine," said Merrill, "I'll have tea without you."

Grace's eyes opened and looked down at Merrill, who squinted up at two glowing orbs where her sister's eyes were the other three hundred sixty-four days of the year.

"The tea's getting cold," said Merrill.

All Aboard!

Brandon Butler

Mandy charged through the mist two steps at a time. Nearing the top of the stairwell, she leapt onto the platform and turned to see the back of the 6:30 to New New York as it left the station, its red and white lights blinking through the haze. *No.* She fell to her knees. *Please God, no.*

Passengers scattered, moving past. They moved in a methodical hurry, an anxious rush that permitted not a single glance down. Fine, whatever. Run. Hide. It wasn't like this town knew to do anything else.

It took a while for the gang to reach her. "You didn't make it?" Karen asked somewhere over her shoulder.

Mandy didn't turn around. "No." She raised her head to look up to the sky, but the early morning was lost in the gray. The platform lay empty and she sighed, lowering her gaze into lingering, shallow pools of rainwater left upon the concrete. "All right," she said, "get the weapons."

More footsteps as everyone headed back down the stairs. Mandy turned as they left to see that only Braxis remained, the great big husky who occasionally left Sammy's side to join hers. She ran a hand through the dog's coarse hair and resisted the urge to nuzzle him as a breeze passed over her face and a pair of boots came into view as she crouched near Braxis. "You're staying?" a voice asked.

She looked up. A large man stood in front of her; tall and brown-skinned, big shoulders packed within a green field jacket. He looked like one of those grizzled war veterans, or an ostensible fan of grizzled war veterans. Stubble ran across his cheeks and chin, and a deep scar trickled down one side of his face. A second marked the base of his throat. "Yeah," she told him.

"You know what happens at seven?"

Mandy swallowed, pushing aside a lock of her curtained, raven-black hair. "Everybody knows."

"Not everyone. Not even close to everyone."

"Well, everyone in town. You from town?"

"I'm from around," the man said, then inclined his head. "Hernandez."

Mandy looked down at Braxis but the husky just looked back at her with big, dumb, happy eyes. She nodded back up at the man. "Mandy," she said.

"Pleased to meet you, Mandy. You should go."

"My friends are coming back. I'll be fine." She paused, giving Hernandez a squinty, guarded look. "My boyfriend's with them."

"Good for you. Leave with him. Grab some coffee, or sex or something. This station's not for you right now."

"I have to take this train," Mandy said, folding her arms. "It's under control."

Hernandez leaned back, his eyes giving her a considered study. "New job?"

Mandy smacked her lips in annoyance. "Yeah."

"Pretty important? First day?"

"Yeah."

"Hallelujah. Productive hands are graceful hands. Now smarten up and catch the next train."

Couldn't this guy give it up? Mandy had half a mind to flip him off, but… she looked past him down the tracks. Nothing there, not yet, just the empty and silent rail line running through a grove of leafless birch. She gritted her teeth. Losing her cool would be the stupid move. She stuck her chin out and stood her ground instead.

Hernandez looked from her to Braxis and back again. "Fine," he said, "fine," and moved away down the platform.

The gang returned soon after. Karen had the crowbar, Ellie the kitchen knife; Francisca brought the family pistol while Moral Support Marky had that rifle borrowed from God-knows-where. And Sammy, oh wow. Sammy had his barbed wire bat, the kick-ass one with the nails driven through. Hard and spiky. You had to love a man who knew how to make violence fun.

Marky looked over towards where Hernandez had edged. "Who's the old guy?" he asked. "He's kind of cute."

"Nobody," said Mandy. She turned to Karen, holding out her hand.

Karen shifted, acting like she didn't have it but Mandy could see the sword right there, strapped to her back. "Can't we talk about this, Mands?" she asked.

Mandy made an exasperated sound and walked behind Karen, unfastening the blade and taking it from her. She unsheathed the first inch of her finest possession, admiring the steel, shining even in comatose morning weather. Satisfied, she slid it back as Ellie handed over her sparring gauntlets. "What's to talk about?" Mandy said. "I missed my train."

"It's my fault; I slept in," said Karen. Her blue eyes darted back and forth behind mousy glasses. "Look, I can fix this. If we take the twelve-oh-four to—"

"Karen, stop. There's no way to program your car for me to make it by nine. Not with what we can afford."

Karen grew flush, blinking. "You can't take the Nightmare. You can't."

"I have to."

"Just listen, there's another way; I've been talking to, I mean…" Karen looked down the tracks then shut her eyes tight, lips pulled back like she was about to cry or bite off her own mouth. She covered it with her hand.

Mandy reached under Karen's glasses, and wiped the tears from her ducts with the heel of her thumb. "Hey. It's okay. We all knew this could happen, if one of us got a job in town. You did your best. Setting alarms can be a bitch, all right? Look… give Ellie the crowbar. Go home."

Karen snapped her head back. "What?"

"Go home. It's okay. We can take it from here."

Karen looked them all over, pulling her open cardigan closer around her chest. "You're kicking me out of the group," she said.

Mandy snapped a finger, pointing it in her face like they

were back in third grade. "Stop saying that. Stop."

"But you won't listen! I think there's…" Karen trailed off, her voice growing weaker as she gave up. Finally, she handed over the crowbar and ran off down the platform stairs.

"You didn't have to be hard on her," Marky said after she was gone.

Mandy silenced him with a look, bracing the sheathed blade between her legs as she twisted on the gauntlets. "I love Karen. But she's no good in a fight."

"*I'm* no good in a fight," Ellie piped up.

"Ellie, I saw you knock down Dan McGee in the middle of Mr. Harlaw's history class after he kept harassing me. I never forget when someone beats me to a punch."

"That was Karen!"

Gauntlets on, Mandy froze. She looked back towards the stairs. "Oh. Right, yeah," she said, and all at once wanted to run back home and stay forever. Jobs in New New York—jobs anywhere—were a big deal, but taking the 7 a.m. Nightmare was one desperate bit of madness. She started taking off the gauntlets when Sammy was suddenly there, pulling her aside with Braxis in tow. "You got this," he said after they were a few feet away.

"Are you kidding? It's a disaster. This was not the plan."

"It was always a flimsy plan. Traffic, sleeping in, it's a tough world out there. Listen, do you want the job?"

Mandy closed her eyes. There in her mind, she saw herself walking marble office hallways, pushing presentations over touchscreens that felt like silk, fetching coffee, and oh, the paycheck! Had you ever seen one? Like precious relics from high finance genies, they bestowed quality food, entertainment, pump-action weaponry; quality *living* to go around. She might even find a house, better than her parents' with property value so low due to their remote location and the hushed, shadowy visits of the Nightmare. A big house with a room for every person that had ever shown enough guts take her side. Bought with actual money. Take that Universal Basic Income script and blow it out your ass.

"Yes," Mandy said as the future passed and faded before her eyes. "Yes, I want it."

Sammy beamed down. They were poor. Maybe not poor like people used to be, but poor enough. Nonetheless, Sammy always looked so clean, so boy-band fresh, smelling like he'd strolled out of the 1980s without a decade to spare. "'Atta girl," he said, "we're here for you. Now come on and take your shot."

And then, as if it had been listening, the 7 a.m. Nightmare pulled into the station without a sound.

Sleek, black and windowless, it shone like Mandy's blade, with ridges that ran up and down between sections, making it look like a long, glass worm. She'd seen drawings before, heard the whispered stories, like the one about the five journalists that came to town and disappeared, one after the other. Or when the National Guard came to blow it clean off its tracks, only to stand down as it approached. The Nightmare always came, always went, and no one dared block its path. Once in the comfort of New New York, it would make its last solemn stop before disappearing to sleep beneath the earth until arising with the dawn of the next day. Nobody could explain it, nobody went near it and absolutely nobody talked about it openly. Not anymore.

It slowed to a halt. Braxis whimpered and bolted from Sammy's side, disappearing down the stairs.

Sammy moved to follow the husky, but Mandy put a padded hand over his chest. Leave it to the dogs to make informed decisions. Removing a gauntlet, she walked up to the train and reached out, tentatively brushing her fingertips along the Nightmare. It looked like glass but felt like flesh; soft and slimy. "Never thought I'd see this up close," she said.

"It's weird," said Ellie. "Mands, you sure about this?"

The doors opened. There were four or five along the train, and the closest revealed a deep red interior with everything beyond the entrance obscured by shadows. Someone stood in the doorway, a young man with sickly, moist skin, staring into the distance with cloudy eyes. He wore a simple pillbox hat that didn't match his unassuming clothes. He just stood there, mouth hanging open.

"Hey," Mandy said. She walked up to the young man and waved a hand in his face. "You okay?"

The guy didn't respond. After a long moment he took off his hat and handed it to Mandy. Then he walked out of the train, staggering across the platform towards the stairs.

"There," said Sammy, "still breathing. Can't be that bad."

Hernandez walked between them and got on board. "You smell better than you think, son," he said, turning around. "It always leaves at least one."

"Who does?" Mandy asked. "How do you know?"

Hernandez opened his jacket. Lined inside were as many weapons as would fit—handguns with ammunition to spare, brass knuckles, knives large and small, and even grenades packed next to a mound of C4. Mandy's mouth dropped open as she resisted the urge to caress and admire each enticing toy. "Because I take this train every day. Last chance to turn around."

Everyone looked to Mandy. She swallowed, then hoisted herself onto the edge of the train. "Look, guys," she said, "I appreciate you being here. But this is my gig. I can't ask—"

She had to step away as Moral Support Marky barreled past. He climbed up onto the train and looked down—as refined as anyone could pretend to be in heavy flannel and his uneven blend of flamboyance and utility with gothic tattoos and painted eyebrows. He shifted the rifle on his shoulder and reached for her, pulling her onto the train with him. "If you're going love, I'm going," he said, then looked at Hernandez. "And shut up, pretty boy. You've been taking the wrong sort of train, if you ask me."

Hernandez ignored him. He inclined his head and, giving Mandy one last lingering glance, disappeared into shadow.

It was quiet inside. Black and red and rosewood-brown, the cabin lay before them, lit by candlelight. Carpets lined the aisles between rows of soft leather seats. Doors to adjacent cars stood on either end, with long drapes where windows should be. Mandy pulled them aside, revealing only wooden paneling. Sammy leaned over a chair. "All aboard the Dracula express," he said.

Mandy looked around. Narrow stairs ran to an upper level. "Let's climb," she said.

Upstairs was the same. Everyone looked to each other and sat down. "No seat belts," Ellie complained.

"The terror deepens," said Mandy, drumming her fingers over the arm of her chair. She took out her phone. Full bars of service—who knew? She pulled up Karen in the contacts list. *Sorry I snapped*, she typed, *on train now. Wish us luck.* Mandy sent it off. Hopefully she'd live to read the response.

"I gotta go to the bathroom," Ellie whined.

Mandy hung her head forward, hair falling into her face. Was it too late to throw herself down the stairs? Stupid misremembered acts of everlasting friendship.

The train lurched forward. Everyone grabbed their armrests as a deep rumbling came from below. It didn't sound like an engine. More like a low moan rising from the grave. Then it fell and rose again and again, creating a rhythm. Mandy felt the momentum building, churning. They were on their way.

Nobody said anything for a long time. The seats were comfortable. You know, if you got past the ever-present lurking sense of abominable evil, it wasn't half bad. "When's the last time anyone took this train?" Ellie said after a while.

"We just met two of them," Francisca hissed.

"No, I mean somebody that went missing. Or someone found dead. I mean, you never hear anything, right? It's never in the news, nobody talks about it. Maybe it's just a weird, shitty train they can't get rid of."

Francisca lolled her head towards Mandy, rolling her eyes so Ellie couldn't see, then turned back. She raised the pistol, pointing it casually towards the ceiling. "Dream your dreams, honey. I'll keep my faith in this while I'm here, thanks."

The lights went out.

Ellie let out a cry, short and shrill. Mandy stood but couldn't see a damn thing. She carefully drew her blade over her head, assuming high guard. All that Kendo better start paying off.

"Quiet!" Marky said, but Ellie kept crying. "Quiet!" There was a rumbling, hard to hear above Ellie's cries, but it grew louder. Like stomping feet pounding up the stairs or down the aisle. Then the shrieking began. Mandy turned one way, then the other, listening as everyone hollered and shouted and pleaded to God.

Snarling. Deep, guttural and feral. A voice rose in a long scream that went on and on before growing weak and ending in a gurgle. Mandy only knew it wasn't Ellie; her contrasting cries had become short, terrorized bursts, like panting agony. Mandy waited. Swing and she might maim any of her closest friends; their swords, guns and bats rendered useless with the simplest trick of sight and sound.

Silence descended. The lights came back up, like a play ready to begin its second act. Ellie cowered in a corner, Marky stood frozen with his rifle pointed at the ceiling, Sammy turned away with his hands over his ears.

And Francisca was gone.

Marky crept into the middle of the train car. Sammy joined him. They didn't always get along, but came together on matters of Mandy—and now, survival. "Did you see where she went?" Sammy asked. Marky shook his head.

Mandy walked over. Francisca's gun lay between streaks of blood on the hardwood floor. She bent down and shoved it into her pocket.

"We have to get off this train," Ellie said, still sobbing.

"A bit late for that," said Mandy. "It doesn't stop 'til New New York." She took a deep breath. "Let's get out of here, at least."

"Downstairs," Sammy said, extending his hand. She took it, smiling. He always knew how to make things better. He held her close as they walked together, though she caught Marky scowling as he struggled to coax Ellie from the floor.

They waited at the bottom of the stairs. "Next car," Mandy said when her friends came down.

"What if Francisca comes back?" Ellie asked.

Mandy didn't dignify that with a response.

The double doors to the next car were tall and ornate, with cloudy panes of glass in the center. She went to open them but Sammy came up, slipping his hands over hers. "Hold on," he said, gently moving her aside. "Could be dangerous."

She stepped back. "This is *my* first day," she reminded him, "*my* job. *My* responsibility."

"Would you rather I sat back and watched you take all the heat?"

Mandy squirmed. She hated questions like this. "Yes," she said. "No. Sometimes?"

"Okay. Sometimes it is. So sometime later, you can get the next one." He opened the doors.

The head of a giant ant burst through and thrust its mandibles into Sammy's chest.

Everyone screamed again. Sammy's legs went limp, his face gaping in shock as he weakly swung his bat while the ant jostled him like a rag doll. Mandy charged, slashing and slashing but her sword just glanced off the creature's tough shell.

Ellie crawled under a chair. Marky backed up, raised the rifle and fired, but missed and hit the top of the door frame. Dust and splinters rained down as blood gushed out of Sammy, soaking the floor. The creature made loud, clicking noises that sounded like a laugh.

Mandy tried pulling Sammy back but the thing had him locked tight in its jaws. "No!" she shouted, hacking away. Gouts of blood splashed onto her face, covering her eyes. "No, no, no, no, no!"

Suddenly an arm pushed her aside as a tall man stepped forward with a sawed-off shotgun in his hand. Hernandez. He pointed his gun into the ant's bulging black eye. "*Trigger warning!*" he roared, blowing a hole that erupted in a yellow splatter on the other side of the creature's head, fist-sized chunks staining the walls. Sammy and the ant fell to the ground.

Mandy leapt over, dragging Sammy back into the cabin, running her hands over his face and hair. His eyes stared blankly. Their pupils did not move. She gazed into them, her face as motionless as his.

"He's gone," Hernandez said, hovering somewhere above.

"He's good," she insisted. She pushed loose folds of his shirt aside, saw the gashed, torn meat of what had been his fine and hairless chest. "He's good. He just... needs a solid time out."

Hernandez let out a sigh. "I told you it would be this way," he said.

Mandy wheeled, grabbing her sword. She swung it into the air between them. "Shut up!" she yelled. "Shut up!" She swung the sword again.

On the third swing Hernandez unsheathed a Bowie knife and blocked her strike. The blades hung there, clashed, one against the other. "Do you want to get out of this alive?" Hernandez asked.

"*I want to get to fucking work!*"

"Good enough. Stick with me, all of you."

"I don't get it," Ellie's dazed and uncomprehending voice rose from beneath her chair. "I mean, why does anyone still use that station? You could build another one, commute from there. It all just seems *clearly* unsafe…"

Marky walked over. He leaned the muzzle of his gun over the still-frozen blades and Mandy pulled hers away from Hernandez's knife. Marky knelt down, putting an arm around her. She clutched at his shoulder and squeezed.

A loud, mechanical screeching filled the air and everyone fell forward. Mandy landed on all fours. The train was slowing. She looked at Hernandez as he braced against a wall. "A shutdown," he said with a grimace. "It does these when it really wants to fuck with you. We have to find the problem and fix it."

"We're not going anywhere," Marky said. The momentum stopped and he stepped in front of Mandy as the train shuddered to a complete stop. "Poking around just got two of us killed."

"Yes. It wants to keep the good times rolling." Hernandez pulled himself off the wall. "I've been through this. It's not going to move until it gets what it wants."

"It can't stay. What about the other trains?"

"It won't move *until it gets what it wants.*"

Mandy exchanged glances with Moral Support Marky. Once upon a time, years ago, everyone thought they were a couple. Teased and teased them. *M & M Enterprises.* And because they were young and didn't know anything, they tried it out a few times until Marky decided het-normative wasn't his slice of life. That was hard. She'd never told him, how hard that was. But not ever having that conversation seemed to let them skip others, allowing them to communicate with the slightest expressions. "Fine," Marky said after a long minute, "we'll go."

Soon they were crawling over what was left of Sammy and the ant into the next car and up through the train, Hernandez in front, Marky in back, and the girls in the middle. Mandy didn't know if the train had slowed or stopped, but she could still hear the moan of the engine somewhere far ahead and deep below.

The cars looked the same until they reached the fourth. Wide and squishy, it heaved with walls of dark, undulating skin. Hernandez stalked inside. Mandy followed. She saw movement ahead, but couldn't make out exactly what was making it.

Hernandez produced a flashlight from his array of tools and weapons. He shone it over a writhing floor, a twitching set of triangular wedges. He held up a hand as the wedges pulled downward, widening into a hole.

"In there?" she asked.

Hernandez nodded. "It wants you."

"How do you know?"

He passed the flashlight beam over the hole, revealing the name 'Miranda' written in scarred flesh along the rim. She looked inside, but saw only darkness. "How is that possible?" she asked. "The tracks are just a few feet down."

"Nothing makes sense in the Nightmare," Hernandez said. "You have to go alone. There'll be trouble if you don't."

"There'll be trouble if I do."

"Yes. But the longer we amuse it, the better our chances."

He handed her the flashlight.

Mandy looked to Ellie. She seemed too weak to look back, staring at the floor, nose running, smelling a little funny, her eyes a flushed mess of tears and anguish. But Marky looked Mandy straight in the eye. His gaze flickered down to the hole, then returned. He nodded, once.

"Right," Mandy said. She stepped over and tapped Ellie on the cheek to snap her back to reality, handing her Francisca's pistol. She drew her sword with her free hand. "Remember," she said, "I love you guys." She turned to Hernandez. "You and I just met, so that can't reasonably apply."

Hernandez shrugged.

"Wish me luck," Mandy said. With that, she braced her arms to her sides and hopped into the hole.

She bent into a squat when she landed at the bottom, nine or ten feet deep, and looked up. The hole was as black looking out as it had been looking in. She lowered her gaze and saw a tunnel stretching ahead. The walls seemed cut from rough black stone, with amber lamps burning in the corners.

The noise of the engine rose. Mandy felt the train's momentum increase as it started moving again, as if accepting her arrival within itself. She took a deep breath of relief, and walked forward.

"*Miranda*," a voice called. She looked back down the tunnel. No one forward, no one back. Oh. One of *those* voices. She tightened her grip on the sword. The voice kept calling, "*Miranda, Miranda, Miranda...*" She spat on the floor. Even

Mom didn't call her Miranda anymore.

The tunnel ascended, its walls smoothing like polished obsidian. Mandy followed, hearing her name with every step.

And then she heard: *"I have a job for you, Miranda."*

"Get in line," she said, "I'm in demand." The tunnel was evening out. It seemed to come to an end just ahead.

With a loud crack, the walls split. No, not split—the top half lifted and pulled away, revealing long and greasy windows. For the first moment since entering the train, Mandy saw daylight. Withered trees, grass and bushes of a lifeless countryside passed below. She walked closer to what had been the end of the tunnel. There seemed to be a panel there, embedded in stone.

"Yes, right there," the voice said. *"Do you see it?"*

The panel had a palm print in its center, surrounded by yellowed spikes, like jutting fangs. "What is it?" she asked. She guessed the voice would respond, seeing as how they seemed to be on a conversational, first-name basis.

"Put your hand there. Become the driver."

"Whose driver?"

"Mine. With the power to summon me to life or lull me to sleep. To jump the bars of these wretched tracks and lead me to roam free upon the earth. Until I find one with the will to claim my helm and make me theirs, I may only dream such sweetened visions."

"And you've chosen me?"

"No. I have a job opening. I am suggesting that you apply."

The voice laughed. *"Many have tried."*

Mandy lowered her sword. The palm print looked exactly the same size as her hand. The pillbox hat the stranger had given her felt suddenly heavy where she'd strapped it to her waist. She had a sudden spark of insight. "Is that why you're doing this?" she asked. "Trying to find someone who has what it takes?"

There was a long pause. *"I experiment,"* the voice finally said. *"Like the great experiment in the underground machine that wrought me from its steely womb, I test by trial and by error. I test by the right of science and laws of nature."*

"You've killed my friends," said Mandy. "And my boyfriend."

"They were weak. You are not."

Mandy stifled a scowl, forcing a sly grin onto her face. She took off a gauntlet and held out a hand, as if sizing the fit. To get it really excited, she asked, "What's the pay?"

Another pause. *"No pay. Only power."*

"Ah." On came the gauntlet. "No pay. Like an intern?"

"Like a Queen."

Mandy shook her head. "You look like slimy shit, you act like slimy shit, and this is one slimy, shitty bribe." Mandy raised her sword. *"And you killed my fucking boyfriend!"*

She drove the weapon into the panel. Black goo spat from the center of the palm like a burst artery. She pulled out the sword and backed away.

"Miranda," the voice began again, but now whispering in anger. *"Miranda, Miranda, Miranda…"* More blackness oozed

from the panel onto the floor. She watched as something rose from it, human-shaped, like a man dipped in tar. *"Miranda, Miranda, Miranda..."*

Mandy flipped the creature off. She fixed her dueling stance. It raised its runny arms and shambled forward.

Something exploded behind her and Mandy staggered to one side. A hole had been blown into the ceiling of the declining tunnel. Marky appeared, crouching through the opening. "Come on!"

She ran. The oily thing tried giving chase but moved slowly and Marky shot a couple bullets into it to slow it further. Mandy jumped into the hole, pulling her legs through as Marky helped her up.

She emerged from the floor of a room raging with gunfire. It was an angular, broad hexagon, with bolts of electricity snapping off its metal walls and singeing the air like the center of a high voltage generator. Hernandez unleashed hell upon more of the black tar creatures as Ellie stood beside him, awkwardly firing away.

"Aim higher!" Hernandez shouted, then looked back. He switched placed with Marky. "You made it," he said.

"Barely."

"What happened? Did it speak to you? Make the offer?"

Mandy took a step back. "How—"

Hernandez moved past, looking into the hole. Then he cried out, shooting back the way she'd come. *"You didn't take the offer?"* he cried.

"It wanted me as its slave!"

"It wanted you as its *master*! Do you know how long I've been trying to get in there and stop this crazy train?"

"How was I supposed to—" Ellie screamed, cutting Mandy off. She was trying to fix a problem with her pistol, helplessly watching an oil creature close in. Mandy dashed forward, crashing into her as she sliced through the thing and half its body slid away. Ellie staggered, firing wildly, careening into the waiting grasp of a second monster. Mandy gasped, reaching out.

Ellie's face looked clouded and half asleep. But her eyes popped open at the last moment, as if realizing peril the instant before it struck. Black, fingerless hands caught her by the head. Sludge ran into her nose, mouth and eyes. Her scream was frozen as blackness sealed over her. Then it caved in as the entire mess dissolved away.

Mandy stumbled as Marky raged, aiming his rifle at the waist and blowing the thing apart. "Come on!" Hernandez cried, stepping up and finishing off the last of the creatures with bursts from his semi-automatic.

They moved through the train. Marky and Hernandez flanked Mandy's every step, eyes watching every corner. Her phone buzzed and she pulled it out in a daze. Text message from Karen. *Good Luck*, it said.

Mandy it shut off. "Which car is safest?" she asked.

No sooner had she spoken than they turned a corner into a room of dead flesh. Corpses spread across the floor and hung from the walls. Each body looked fresh, limbs pinned against one another or swaying in the air. Blood smeared every open space with an overwhelming stench that nearly knocked Mandy over. Marky reached out to steady her.

A man stood in the middle, alive in the midst of the carnage. He had a familiar posture, an effeminate air, and it took a moment for Mandy to realize it was Marky. She looked up and saw her greatest friend stare at himself, shock stamped onto his face and the core of his being. The other Marky smiled and raised an arm, pointing.

Marky pushed Mandy aside, raised his rifle and fired, but his twin was already gone. Then he cried out, dropping to his knees. Mandy was there instantly. She tried sitting Marky back as he tilted his head, his mouth hanging open and his eyes, milky white, staring out blindly. He turned toward her and gnashed his teeth into a smile. "You weren't the only one," he said.

She blinked. She let go of him and stood, dropping Marky like dead weight into the ocean. He kept staring. "I had to find out," he said, "I had to be sure of what I was. There was a girl before you. And another after."

"Shut up," she said and then, repeating in a scream, *"shut up!"*

"And, to be honest, you were only second best."

Hernandez hit Marky over the back of the head, knocking him out. Mandy's entire body shook.

Before tears could rain down her face, a roar came from above. Another impossible black hole appeared in the ceiling and some new terror pulled itself from the center. Pale green with maybe a dozen legs encased in exoskeleton, it looked like a cross between a spider and praying mantis, with a mouth wielding two sets of sharp incisors and a long red tongue wriggling through the middle. It let out a hiss and turned toward them.

Hernandez dropped to one knee, shooting. "Take him!" he said, pushing Marky toward Mandy.

She took Marky's limp body by the arm. "What about you?"

Hernandez shot off one of the beast's legs and it reeled, falling to the floor. He looked back and winked. "I'll be okay," he said. "I do this every day."

Mandy nodded. She grabbed Marky and pulled, dragging him foot by foot, leaving the roar of gunfire and rabid shrieks behind.

They fell backward into the adjacent car, door sliding shut. She rolled Marky to the side. Funny; this looked like the cabin they first entered, when everyone was still alive. She took a breath, shut her eyes and opened them again. The lights went out. She groaned.

And then the voice once more, whispering from the dark. "*Miranda, Miranda, Miranda... you can always re-apply, Miranda.*"

The train stopped. The moan of the engine fell as the lights came back on. Everything went quiet.

Mandy didn't move. Finally, Marky stirred. She got him up, drew herself under his arm to support his weight. A door slid open from the side of the car and they staggered out.

Sunlight, blindingly bright. They fell into an empty station, the 7 a.m. Nightmare sitting idle behind them. All around she saw shafts of skyscrapers and heard the muted bustle of New New York. Marky squatted on the station floor, holding his head. She turned and watched as the long and evil worm pulled away, churning into a waiting tunnel past the end of the platform. She watched until the very last of it disappeared and was gone.

Marky got to his wobbly feet. She looked at him, wiping mascara streaks from her eyes. "Was that true?" she asked. "About those girls?"

"Was what true?"

"Forget it. Let's go."

They exited onto a busy street, passing lines of commuters awaiting any next train that wouldn't also send them on a personal trip to hell. Someone stood alone on the opposite side of the road. Karen. Braxis sat beside her.

Mandy stopped, barely able to move. "How…"

Karen ran up and threw her arms around her. Braxis barked and leapt up, leaning into Marky. "You're alive!" Karen said. "You're alive, you're alive! What happened to…" she looked into Mandy's eyes, and her gaze fell to the ground. "Oh."

Mandy let them both take a moment. "How did you get here?" she asked after it had passed.

"That's what I was trying to say! I wasn't sure, but I read about a monorail service opening in the next township. I checked and sure enough, it was running. But by then you were on your way…" Her eyebrows pushed together in the center of her forehead. "I'm sorry. Sammy was such a nice guy."

"Yeah," Mandy took off the gauntlets and wrung her hands. "And Francisca was good for a laugh. I'll miss them. Um…" she paused, thinking. "How was the ride?"

"Terrible. Getting Braxis on was a pain, the entire thing was packed. Couldn't get a seat. Had to use handlebars."

Mandy made a face. Handlebars? "Oh, fuck *that*," she said, looking to Marky, then at the clock on her phone. Not quite half past eight. There was time to grab a bite, if they hurried. She looked down and saw the stranger's hat still strapped to her belt. Sun shining on her face, she looped her gauntlets next to it and took each of her friends by the arm. "All right, guys," she said, "buck up. My new life starts in half an hour. I've got a feeling I'm in for a lovely day."

Vlad's Incorruptible Soul

W. T. Paterson

"Hi, my name is Vlad and I'm an alcoholic," said the pale man with long, stringy black hair. His eyes were sunken and his flesh was starting to sag. He was a vampire too, but no one at the meeting knew that.

"Hi, Vlad," the room answered back in unison. People sat in a poorly formed circle, tired and dressed in anything but their Sunday best. The group came in their Thursday best— the exhausted carelessness of a well-worn button-up and jeans that could use a wash. Few took the time to shower. Fewer took the time to even scrub their hands clean.

Clean…what an unnatural concept.

"Even though my name is Vlad, I prefer my middle name, Terry," the man spoke. His voice had the lilt of a southern dance and the dark undertones of Eastern Europe.

The fluorescent-lit room held the air captive with such a stranglehold that the idea of an oscillating fan became an obsessive fantasy. It smelled like old wood rot mixed with stale coffee and pastries. These weren't the kind of pastries that people woke up craving, either.

Craving…what an odd idea.

If a pregnant woman craves peanut butter, she's given it. If a man craves a drink, he's a monster.

People sat with their arms crossed and staring at the

floor. No one truly wanted to be there, but they had become addicted to being there.

"Will you share tonight, Terry?" Donald asked. His comb-over was a pathetic grasp at normalcy and drew even more attention to the liver spots. Yet, he had a wonderful way of bringing out the best in people if they could get past his drooping Deputy Dog jowls and nearly exploded red nose.

"Actually, call me Vlad."

Vladimir Metairie Johnson tongued the canines at the front of his mouth, wondering if tonight would be the night he'd lose it entirely.

"We're here for you," Donald nodded.

"I'd like to talk tonight about the weight of a soul," Vlad started. "As many of you know, I've been using on and off for nearly my whole life. I've lost friends (Jamie Nuulsen, throat ripped out, drunken bet. Helena Silvio, promised life eternal, chickened out/bled out), I've lost family (Mama Dragomedov, outlived. Papa Johnson, sunrise battle during the March Against the Unholy), and somewhere along the way I lost myself (see above). It used to weigh me down. Still does. How many people here have dreamt about a pure soul? A true, golden soul?"

The room raised their hands in staggered pops.

"Well the thing about gold is that it's incorruptible. Gold only exists as gold. Can't combine other elements to make it. And for this reason, gold is heavy. I started wondering that if my soul was cleansed and turned to gold—maybe I'd still feel weighed down. Maybe there's no escaping the choices I've made. Maybe being pure means being weighed down by the choices we refused or would not make."

Empty, slow nods went around the room. The dark windows of the church's Rec Center reflected the night like mirrors.

"So it sounds like you're saying we have to accept ourselves as faulty? That we are corruptible creatures full of imperfections and false altruism?"

"What I'm saying is that we need to love ourselves for who we are, for what we are, and not for what we do. Or something like that. I don't know. It sounded cool in my head, but then I started talking..."

"Better than a silver soul," said a new voice from the doorway. A man stood in a long trench coat stained with blood and feces. He wore a wide-brimmed hat, aviator glasses, combat boots, and pants typically reserved for the bargain bin at Hot Topic (all black, too many pockets, zippers that led to nothing, and chains that connected to other chains).

He was clearly wasted.

"Oh, here we go..." Vlad whispered under his breath, and put his head in his hands. Of course Hugo had shown up. *Supernatural* on the CW must have just aired the finale.

"Judas sold out Christ for thirty pieces of silver. When Christ was crucified, Judas attempted to repent for his sin and return the silver to the priests and elders that had paid him. When they wouldn't accept the return, Judas threw the silver on the temple floor and left, intent on hanging him-self. But he found he could not die, and that sunlight burned his exposed skin, and there was an insatiable thirst for inno-cent blood. Silver became a curse upon his flesh. Also, do you have a bathroom? I think I just shit my pants."

"Down the hall, second door on the left. First door is just a closet. I only say that because we've had issues before," Donald said. "And sir? It looks like you may benefit from our group here. If you'd like to come back, you're more than welcome but I do ask that you refrain from passing any judgment. This is a judgment-free zone."

"Ask this monster why he couldn't carry a soul of silver," Hugo grunted, pinching his cheeks shut. He waited a moment for a reply, then excused himself to hobble towards the restroom. "Oh, second door. Right," his voice bounced back.

"You're not a monster," Donald said kindly, putting a gentle hand on Vlad's shoulder. "You're just as God made you."

"Eeeh, let's not say anything we can't take back," Vlad said, then grabbed his coat to leave. He wished them all well and said he'd be back in a few days, much to Donald's disap-pointment.

On his way out, he pushed open the bathroom door and forced the front fangs to emerge. He locked the door quietly before kicking through the flimsy stall and grabbing Hugo by the collar.

"You need to leave me alone!" he shouted in a voice that

sounded demonic and hollow.

But Hugo had fallen asleep on the toilet, the back of his coat filling the bowl and soaking up excrement. When Vlad let him go, Hugo's head lolled to the side and he remained completely passed out. He was the sorriest excuse for a vampire hunter this generation had ever seen.

Excuses…what a peculiar way to justify bad choices.

It was Mardi Gras in New Orleans. The lawlessness and chaos brought out the creepers and weirdos in droves. But they were a different breed than the creepers and weirdos at Comic-Con. These folks still hid behind masks, but let their dark desires run rampant instead of fantasizing about space travel or superpowers. The flash of a nip meant acquiring plastic beads and a thousand drunken propositions. It was hell for the local PD.

Vlad shouldered his way down Bourbon Street, feeling the urge to use as people shoved past him smelling like vodka tonic, or whiskey sour, or Miller Lite—you know, the beer that truly marks a special occasion in a destination event. He noticed Officer Danika Pebbles in a side alley. She had two twenty-something females sitting, handcuffed, both of whom were spouting venomous rhetoric. He could hear it over the swing-jazz marches being played in the street.

"This is Mardi Gras! People are *supposed* to show their tits!" one said.

"This is a violation of my American constitutional rights!" the other slurred.

"Oh?" Pebbles amusedly replied. "Which amendment guarantees you the right to pull out a double-headed dildo in a public place and use it for tips?"

"Because I'm a *human* and I am *sexual!*" the first said.

"It's called *liberation!*" the second battled.

"Hmm. Still not convinced."

"Oh, like you've never showed *your* tits, you prude."

"Yeah! Flash them puppies! Woooo!"

From the street, a separate woo echoed back in. Vlad leaned against the wall and watched as Pebbles radioed for an escort.

"We're not escorts!" the first girl yelled. "We are students at Brown University. Pre-Med! Ever heard of it? And my dad is going to…"

"Oh my god…where is my phone?! It was in my bra, but I'm not wearing it anymore!"

At this, the second girl started to sob.

"You need to let us out! She lost her phooone!" the first started to plead.

Two more officers came and collected the girls, who continued to argue that they needed to be let free to find the missing phone. Less than a minute later, they both got tazed when they started to spit on the men who were gently leading them to the drunk tank.

"Oh, to be young again," Vlad said, stepping out of the shadows and trying his best to be smooth. He was nervously laughing. "Forever young. What a world that would be."

"*Je-sus!*" Officer Pebbles said, spinning around and

putting her hand on her weapon. "Vlad...how long have you been standing there? You scared the crawdads outta me."

"Long night, huh?"

"It goes the way it goes," the woman said, pushing her palms against the sides of her short blonde hair. Vlad knew she was a mother, and she carried herself like a mother, but she hadn't given up on her body yet. She was still athletic and bragged about doing Jiu Jitsu, a far cry from most of the other middle-aged mothers Vlad met.

"Let me get you off. Maybe we can time what breakfast... our breakfast...wait...what *time* do you get..."

Pebbles smiled sullenly, and Vlad could feel the rejection marching towards him with more force than a rainbow float of half-naked bartenders.

"Vlad, you're a nice boy. I mean that. But we've had this discussion before. You were the main suspect in a *multiple* homicide case. I'm a cop. People like us...we were never meant to be."

"I *was* the main suspect, but the lack of evidence...or bodies..."

"Can't shake that stigma. People talk. Put yourself in my shoes. I'm sorry, but it's never going to happen. Maybe in another lifetime." She smiled. The radio on her shoulder buzzed and when she cocked her head the carotid artery in her neck pulsed like an EDM beat inside porcelain speakers.

The urge was emerging again.

"Be careful what you wish for," he frowned, clenching

his knuckles to keep from losing control.

"10-4" Pebbles said, then turned to Vlad. "Stay safe out there tonight, lots of creepers and weirdos. Gotta run."

She stepped out of the alley and immediately accosted a topless woman with sagging breasts painted like Snoopy.

The thing that no one ever told Vlad about being a vampire was that rejection never hurt less. It always stung, even after 400 years. The human condition was improved through companionship, even if the human condition was molested into life eternal through bloodlust and murder.

He knew it wouldn't last with Danika Pebbles, that nothing ever lasted, but he also knew better than to *not* try. But trying inevitably led to failure, and failure led to self-doubt. Self-doubt led to a heavyset, aging frat bro wearing a backwards hat, pissing down at the far end of the alley. He was pissing on his own shoes and woo-ing at no one.

Vlad only knew one thing that would take away the sting of rejection, the sting of loneliness, and the sting of wandering the earth beneath the moonlight, unable to live and die like his peers.

He needed a drink.

Vlad felt his canines grow and sharpen at the thought like unholy boners. His eyes narrowed, and his feet felt lighter. He barely had to move before he was upon the man and smashing his skull against the bricks so hard that teeth tinkled to the cement like gravel. He bit once on the thick neck and took a sip of the blood rich with booze and felt his world regain order. Everything made sense again. Why had he ever sworn it off, he wondered. Yet, that one taste demanded a thousand more.

In the next moment, he leapt up with such force that both he and the large man were airborne and headed for a rooftop away from public view.

For the rest of the evening, Vlad watched the parades from the roof until every last drop of blood was exhumed from the bro. He smiled and danced under the moonlight, feeling the false sense of happiness surround him like the warmth of whiskey.

Below, the world marched on, paying no mind to the macabre rooftop where a (now) decapitated head was getting defiled by a 400-year-old creature that sang a woeful song about lost love, and a police officer named Pebbles.

When dusk settled in the following night, Vlad awoke hung-over and pissed off. He wasn't in his apartment, but rather Jordan Plummet's Love Palace. Jordan was Vlad's Original and the two had traveled to New Orleans together posing as Acadians. Jordan had also introduced Vlad to blood coursing with booze, drugs, and virginity.

"After the first porking, the blood physically changes. You can taste it. It's more bitter," he'd say.

"We're calling it 'porking' now?"

"The good stuff is the pure stuff. Remember that."

When Vlad finally had his first taste—a young Creole boy named Marcel, he couldn't believe the difference.

"I'm obsessed!" he said, mouth dripping with warm

blood that steamed in the moonlight.

"Pass the dutchie, brotha!" Jordan replied, and together they sucked the life out of the kid whose eyes became permanently frozen in a state of shock.

Waking up in the Love Palace was a cause for alarm. It was a house of ill repute where men and women came to find their jollies. They'd also find an untimely end to their unremarkable lives.

The people who frequented the Love Palace were the type of people who thought it was a good idea to visit places like the Love Palace. Lonely, ego driven, and desperate, they'd knock the secret knock (shave and a haircut), pay in cash, and sign in with an alias to earn customer loyalty points. The majority of people who went were on something, too. They were stoned out of their minds on hydroponic weed, did key bumps in the alley, or took pills from a 6th-year high-schooler outside who only answered to the name Joey Sabotage.

The customer loyalty program was listed as such:
After the 3rd visit, get a free diddlin'.
After the 5th visit, free knobbin'.
After the 10th visit, free cheesy breadsticks.

No one got to ten, though. Around visit 7 or 8, Jordan sank his teeth and the people with fake names and drug-driven motives disappeared quietly into the night while new customers showed up. Whether it was perfect or tragic that no one ever went looking didn't matter because the end result was the same.

"Why does my mouth taste like…a soft…strawberry cloud?" Vlad asked, finding Jordan passed out across two naked and exsanguinous bodies. "Did I score some V-Blood last night?"

"Dawg, you think V cards pass through these doors? Only freaks with the kinky shit. And they call *us* monsters."

"What am I tasting?" he asked, clicking his tongue trying to re-ignite the taste buds.

"No bullshit…a zebra. I don't know where you found one or how you got it here, but you straight up ganked a zebra and sucked it dry in front of like four of my customers. And no bullshit, they paid out the ass to watch you do it."

"Those four right there?"

"Thems the ones. If you weren't making me so much money, I'd say you had a problem. But hey, you do you."

Reality came rushing in like a rugby player's stiff-arm. How was he going to explain this to his rehab group?

Hey everyone, I lapsed. I knew I had a problem when I stole a zebra from a zoo and sucked it dry in front of people so my friend could make some extra cash.

An even more startling realization occurred. That's *exactly* what he *had* to say if he had any shot of getting better. Radical candor. Brutal honesty.

Well, almost.

If he explained he was a vampire, then he'd be dragged outside and crucified. It was literally written into the bylaws of the New Orleans AA chapter. Some idiot in recovery probably thought it was a riot.

It wasn't.

There was a fine line between honesty, and choosing not to reveal specific facts. If Vlad caved and revealed his true nature and they put him on the cross, his father would have died in vain. That simply wasn't an option.

"I know you've changed, son," his father said, the night before the March Against the Unholy. "They're coming for people like you because they don't understand people like you. But you're my son, and that's all I have to know. So I'll be right there fighting against them."

"I'm gonna miss you, Dad," Vlad told him, for the first and last time.

After the march became a massacre and bloodbath, Vlad knelt in the ankle-deep blood, slurping up the remains and promising that one day he'd get better. He'd been stabbed a number of times, once with a gold-tipped spear in an unsuccessful attempt to save his father, and once in the arm with a knife lathered in garlic butter.

After hundreds of years the wounds healed, but the Day of Atonement still hadn't come, no matter how promising the times seemed.

"Brosef," Jordan said from across the room. "If you decide you're gonna get clean, and then decide you're gonna fall off the bandwagon, just give me a heads up. As much money as you made me last night, we both know money ain't shit compared to friendship, yeah? We've gotta be golden. Incorruptible in the face of adversity. Because we are adversity personified. Your struggle is my struggle."

"Gold is heavy. Maybe our friendship weighs us down."

"Being weighed down isn't a bad thing. It keeps us grounded, ya know? Pretending there's order in chaos so that we don't lose ourselves in the abyss. Yo, you slam that cop yet or what?"

"I doubt it's gonna happen."

"You sure? She stopped by looking for you last night. Not in uniform."

"It's probably because I stole a zebra."

"Ohhh, that explains all those 'not so black and white' puns. You know what? She's actually on track for a free diddlin'."

Vlad looked up, amazed.

"I didn't realize she came here…"

"She's a human, homie. She's not exempt from temptation and curiosity. I'd have told you sooner, but I have a rigorous NDA which I take very seriously."

"If she comes back asking for me, please please please let me know."

"Will do. You heading to a meeting or something?"

"Kind of. So there's this guy who's been trying to kill me forever, but he just...is bad at it. I think I need to confront him. Give him the old 'jab a stake or leave a wake' moment."

"Be careful. Sometimes those slippery bastards are crafty."

Vlad nodded and ran a finger through his thick, dark hair as he left. It was matted with dried blood and zebra bits.

Hugo was walking down Frenchman Street with a gym bag slung over his shoulder. His hair was cut short and his glasses were gone. Brand new tennis shoes absorbed the weight of his steps.

"Turning everything around, I see," Vlad said from an alleyway. The hum of the streetlights was almost drowned out by the thump of zydeco swing from a nearby dive bar.

"Last night, I hit bottom," Hugo said, keeping his eyes down and continuing to walk forward. "That group of yours found me and listened. Actually listened. I was able to be honest with myself for the first time in years, and you know what happened? They accepted me for who I was, faults and all."

The fire inside of Vlad turned to rage.

"So you hijacked *my* group to save yourself, you coward."

"I was in a bad place, Vlad. I thought I'd never escape the shadow of my father, never live up to his legacy, never plunge a stake through the heart of an unholy abomination. Last night I learned that that's OK. I don't have to live up to my father's expectations. We're different people, me and him. Sure, a kill here and there would be nice, but my life is my own. Not his. Not anyone else's. All the mistakes I've made, well, I need to own them. So I'm sorry for always trying to murder you with weak attempts at assassination."

Vlad could relate to everything Hugo was saying in some

capacity. While he didn't feel the burden of living in his father's shadow, he felt the burden of outliving everyone he's ever been close to. He felt the sting of death at the corner of his lips every time he smiled. Worst of it all, he had seen the world grow and change so much, while he was cursed to always remain the same. Forever trapped in a state of stasis, the vampire was chained to a world that would rather not acknowledge his existence.

"Where are you going? Shouldn't you be hunting me?" he asked Hugo.

"I'm going to Jiu Jitsu. Officer Pebbles invited me. She said I had a lot of potential. A guy my size with my agility could be a great training partner, she said. And she's got a hot little mom bod."

"You stay away from her!" Vlad warned. "Pebbles has a good soul. A companion's soul. Even if I only get a decade or two in with her, it will have been worth it. So back off!"

"You know, if I were still hunting you I'd know exactly how to push your buttons. I'd know who to go after for leverage. But now, after one meeting with AA, I forgive you. A life of anger and rage is no life at all. I forgive you, Vlad. And I forgive myself. And that's the truth because I understand the value of honesty. I'm not in shape. I have a long way to go to undo the years of bad diets and habits, but at least I'm able to admit that. I can't expect honesty from others if I can't even look inside myself for it."

Hugo's words sliced into Vlad worse than a stake through the heart. It wasn't because he felt left behind by the world, or because there was nothing left that he could tangibly cling onto, but rather that Hugo was right. He had kept his true self a secret for hundreds of years and that type of weight created the workings of a living hell.

When officer Pebbles came around the corner wearing compression shorts and a sky blue sports bra, Vlad knew that life wasn't going to get any easier.

"Hey Hugo!" the woman said, giving him a playful hug. "Oh, Vlad. I didn't see you there. You good?"

"I heard through the grapevine that you were looking for me," Vlad said, trying to chuckle over his awkwardness. "You know grapes are the basis for wine. So the grapevine will become the grape-wine. Or the great-wine!"

"Do you know anything about a missing zebra?" she said, her tone suddenly less playful and more authoritative.

"A what now?"

"Or about a decapitated body found on a rooftop above Bourbon Street?"

"N—no why would I know about…"

"Can you tell me your whereabouts between the hours of 11 p.m. and 4 a.m. last night?"

"I saw you and I went home!" Vlad pleaded, feeling the moment run through his fingers like dripping muscle sinew. Hugo wasn't even taking pride in the grilling. Instead, he looked concerned.

"I stopped in at Jordan Plummet's Love Palace and he gave me a different story," Pebbles said. "And I wasn't there for the reasons it sounds like. He's a known associate of yours."

"Oh. Guess you were just…diddlin' around looking for answers."

Pebbles' cheeks flushed red and she looked down quickly.

"It's my duty to follow any hard leads—that came out wrong—I'm obligated to diddle around in—hold up…"

"I get it. You have needs," Hugo said, putting a steady hand on her shoulder.

"How about we never say that again, sound good?" Pebbles replied, peeling his paw away. "Swing by my office tomorrow, Vlad. We need to have a chat. A real heart to heart."

"And remember, Vlad," Hugo began. "Honesty allows your soul to soar. It frees it from the crushing weight of our own secrets."

Pebbles smiled at Hugo and motioned with her head that they should get going to class. They didn't even say goodbye to the man in the alley who was pondering the idea that maybe rock bottom wasn't one singular event. Maybe it was ripping out Pebble's eyes and drinking Hugo's sweet, sweet virgin blood. Maybe it was that the only two people he considered friends aside from Jordan only wanted him to suffer. Or maybe it was doing nothing at all and letting the natural order restore itself.

"Not my style," Vlad said, and used his inhuman speed and strength to pull them both up onto a rooftop for the most heinous of defilings. Not even dental records could be used to ID the corpses by the time he was finished with them.

Donald had corralled the meeting into its usual circle. The folks there desperately held onto their paper cups filled with lukewarm coffee. Each was engaged in a fierce battle to reclaim their soul from the grip of an unseen beast. Their only salvation came from the courage to call it by its real name.

Addiction.

Vlad came stumbling in and slumped into a chair. A noticeable air of unease puffed from the inhabitants like an A-bomb of 'here we go again'.

"Vlad, welcome back," Donald said, doing his best not to let the throbbing vein in his forehead show. Even though these meetings were about recovery, they were also about discipline. "Is there anything you'd like to tell us?"

The vampire looked around the room and saw the types of people he continuously targeted. He saw the sad faces of bad decisions and consequences of regret. He saw decaying human flesh with even more rotten souls.

Vlad couldn't relate to them. He never could. Even though they all had more in common than any would care to admit, he forever felt alienated by his burden.

"I do have something to say," he started. The fluorescent lights illuminated the imperfect floors with beams too far apart, and chairs barely holding it together after decades of abuse. "I have a problem and I can't stop using. No matter what I try, I always find myself hungry for just one sip. And one sip leads to another, and another, and another, and before I know it—I'm fucking the neck of a decapitated corpse. Figuratively speaking."

The room nodded in consolation relating to moments in their own lives where they lost control of the outcome.

"What else?" Donald asked. He crossed his legs and leaned forward. This could be the breakthrough they've all been waiting for. "Speak your truth, Vlad. We're listening. Rehabilitation cannot begin without honesty."

"I've been in love more times than I can count," Vlad said. "And it always ends the same. They get to know the real me and it freaks them out. Or they don't even give me a shot because at one time in my life I was a 'suspect' in a 'multiple homicide'. It's like no matter what I do, I can't shake the stigma of being different. I don't fit into a box, and I never have. The only box I'll ever fit into is my casket."

The room nodded again. A man in a trucker hat with three-day-old stubble scratched his arm and chuckled to himself.

"Do you want to talk about how it felt being accused of something you weren't? I know you've spoken before about the guilt and torment of that homicide investigation. The lingering effects are still very much alive. Maybe speak to those feelings."

"Fine. Let's say I did do it. Let's say I've killed people. I am a monster without any remorse who loves bloodshed and the macabre. If I lived a thousand lives, that's a part of me that would never change."

To Vlad's shock, he wasn't met with disinterest or terror, he was met with mild applause. And the applause felt good. It felt healing.

"Keep going," Donald said.

"Sometimes I kill because I'm sexually frustrated. Sometimes I kill because I'm bored. And sometimes I kill because people are idiots and it's the only way I can feasibly get through the day-to-day grind."

More mild applause.

"I want to commend you for your bravery here. I'm a trained counselor with years of experience, specifically on the idea of mapping. I want you to ponder something for a moment. When you say 'kill', is it possible that you mean 'use'? Is the killing you refer to symbolic of the actions you commit unto yourself?"

Louder applause. Perhaps the breakthrough was actually coming.

"I use because I choose to use. I take my life into my own hands and yeah, I don't always make the best choices, but sometimes a man's gotta do what a man's gotta do!"

Rising applause.

"You're finally letting your guard down, Vlad. Keep this momentum up."

"Four hundred years! That's how long I've been trapped in this body. Literally! I'm older than the internet. Older than television. Older than the telephone. Older than both world wars. Combined!"

"I've felt the same way. Using made me live lifetimes of loneliness," the man in the trucker hat said, as he began to weep.

"So maybe I'm done hiding. Maybe it's time to reveal to the world who I really am!"

"Say it, Vlad. Say it out loud so that we can all share in your achievement here today."

Before he could, trucker hat man stood up.

"My name is Scott Grainey and I'm a recovering alcoholic."

Another.

"My name is Julia Po and I'm a struggling but recovering alcoholic with a history of substance abuse."

And another.

"My name is Miguel Santiago, and I am an alcoholic who will no longer let my disease define my life!"

The crowd was being whipped into a frenzy. The participants were hooting and hollering for each other as they rose with honesty to reclaim their identity.

"My name is Vlad," the man said, "and I'm an alcoholic. But I'm also a vampire!"

He pulled his lips back and forced his fangs to grow. His soul finally began to feel free, lifted from the burden of secrets.

The room stopped clapping and fell into a horrified, deathly silence.

"Oh...I wish you hadn't told us that," Donald said, hiding his face behind a hand. "I really wish you hadn't done that."

"But…you said…"

"I know. I know. It's partially my fault, but I'm also not… like you. None of us here are…like you. And you've read the bylaws in our handbook. I'm sorry, pal, but if we're to get better, we *all* need to follow the rules."

Scott and Julia and Miguel stood up and grabbed Vlad by the arms, pinning him to the floor. The others in the room started smashing through the wooden tables to pick up makeshift stakes or wrapping their shirts around the points to create torches. The alcohol inside of the sweat-stained cloth created an ease for the fire to leap from a candle and ignite the stick.

"You told me to be honest! Everyone did! I'm being honest, and now you punish me for it?!"

"Honesty with yourself is one thing. Honesty with your therapist is another. Honesty with your AA group is another. There are levels to this thing."

Vlad was dragged outside where a bench was kicked apart and reconstructed into a crucifix. He was hoisted onto it and bound in place.

Yet amidst all the chaos, coming clean did help. For the first time in over 400 years, he felt lighter. He felt like admitting who he was somehow made him stronger. It made his soul shine like gold in the morning sun.

"Go ahead. Kill me. When you do, know that I've won because to vanquish me, you had to become me. We're all users, abusers, and lost souls looking for redemption. Well, not me. I know that a fiery demise awaits, and that's OK.

Light me up!"

Scott and Donald held their torches to the bottom of Vlad's impaled feet. The flames leapt onto his pants and spread faster than the warmth of whiskey. In a matter of seconds, Vlad was fully engulfed in fire, where he roared with laughter as his pale skin and hair fell off in thick, smoldering chunks. His jaw fell slack and open, and his neck began to droop.

In another matter of moments, there was only a skeleton. A moment after that, there was just ash. Vlad had burned far faster than a non-vampire human and, to celebrate, the meeting went back inside for some coffee and pastries to toast to the death of the secret monster that had been plaguing them for years.

It was Donald who took one final moment to survey the scene and noticed the curious relic at the bottom of the cross.

There, shining in the light of the fire was a small puddle of gold. He wasn't sure how he knew, but Donald believed it to weigh exactly 21 grams.

"Huh," he said. "Maybe that old bastard was onto something."

He let the gold cool, picked up the chunk and put it into his pocket, then went inside to celebrate the night with a raspberry Danish and some Sleepy Time tea.

Gold—what an odd thing to model a soul after.

About the Authors

Skyler Goff

Murder Sandwich

Skyler Goff is a novelist, playwright, actor, and educator who lives in Asheville, NC with his lovely bride, Ashleigh. When he isn't writing he enjoys teaching theatre, escape room building, and zombie survival classes to middle schoolers.

Andrew Johnston

Overdue Notice

Born in rural western Kansas, Andrew Johnston discovered his Sinophilia while attending the University of Kansas. Subsequently, he has spent most of his adult life shuttling back and forth across the Pacific Ocean. He is currently based out of Hefei, Anhui province. He has published short fiction in Nature: Futures, the Arcanist, and Mythic.

Website: www.findthefabulist.com.

Alyssa Eckles

Bad Dates and Dragons

Alyssa Eckles is a speculative fiction writer with stories in DreamForge Magazine, Shoreline of Infinity, and A Flash of Silver-Green: Stories of the Nature of Cities. She also writes for American Greetings, mostly funny birthday cards you can't send to Grandma. When she's not putting pen to paper, Alyssa likes running, grabbing a bowl of pho, and planning elaborate vacations she'll never take. She lives in Cleveland, Ohio with too many books and her cats, Libel and Poe.

Website: www.alyssaeckles.com

Twitter: @alyssaeckles

George Nikolopoulos
The Haunting of Peruvius Corcorant

George Nikolopoulos is a member of the Codex Writers' Group. His short stories have been published in over 60 magazines and anthologies including Galaxy's Edge, Nature, Daily Science Fiction, Factor Four, Best Vegan SFF, and The Year's Best Military & Adventure SF. He lives in Athens, Greece, and when he's not writing he is, among other things, an actor, a civil engineer, a husband and a father. He wishes he could write more, read more, travel more, play more computer games, and spend more time with cats.

Website: www.georgenikolopoulos.wordpress.com

Facebook: www.facebook.com/nikolop

Twitter: @g_nikolop

Eric J. Guignard
It Came from Mail Order

Eric J. Guignard has twice won the Bram Stoker Award, been a finalist for the International Thriller Writers Award, and is a multi-nominee of the Pushcart Prize for his works of dark and speculative fiction. He has over one hundred stories and non-fiction author credits appearing in publications around the world; has edited multiple anthologies (including the current series, The Horror Writers Association's HAUNTED LIBRARY OF HORROR CLASSICS with co-editor Leslie S. Klinger); and created an ongoing series of author primers championing modern masters of the dark and macabre, EXPLORING DARK SHORT FICTION through his own press, Dark Moon Books. His latest books are his short story collection, THAT WHICH GROWS WILD (Cemetery Dance Publications, 2018) and novel, DOORWAYS TO THE DEADEYE (JournalStone, 2019).

Website: www.ericjguignard.com
Blog: ericjguignard.blogspot.com
Twitter: @ericjguignard

Jeff Strand
Captain Pistachio's Charming Rampage

Jeff Strand is a four-time finalist (and zero time winner, but he lost to Stephen King *twice*) for the Bram Stoker Award. His 40+ books include PRESSURE, DWELLER, MY

PRETTIES, DEAD CLOWN BARBECUE, EVERYTHING HAS TEETH, and A BAD DAY FOR VOODOO. He lives in Atlanta, Georgia, but please don't show up uninvited after nightfall.

Website: www.JeffStrand.com

Twitter: @JeffStrand

Santiago Eximeno
Your Diabolical Baby

Santiago Eximeno is a Spanish genre writer who has published several novellas and collections, mainly of horror literature. His work has been translated to English, Japanese, French, and Bulgarian. UMBRIA, his award-winning Spanish language horror short story collection will be published in English in 2019 by Independent Legions Publishing.

Website: www.eximeno.com

Twitter: @santiagoeximeno

Sean Logan
Night Stockers

Sean Logan's stories have appeared in more than forty publications, including America Gothic Short Stories, Black Static, Supernatural Tales, and Dark Visions Vol. 1. He lives in northern California with his lovely wife, a matching set of newborn twins, and a giant white Kuvasz that may be part polar bear.

C L Raven
Dying Art

C L Raven are identical twins and mistresses of the macabre. They're horror writers because 'bringers of nightmares' isn't a recognised job title. They write novels, short stories, comics, and film scripts. Their work has been published in magazines and anthologies in the UK, USA, and Australia. A story of theirs was published in The Mammoth Book of Jack the Ripper, which makes their fascination with him seem a little less creepy. They've worked on several indie horror films as crew and reluctant actors and have somehow ended up with lead roles in the forthcoming indie horror film School Hall Slaughter. In their spare time, they hunt ghosts, host a horror radio show, look after their animal army, and try to look impressive with polefit. Their attempts at gymnastics should never be spoken about.

Website: www.clraven.wordpress.com

Twitter: @clraven

William West
Tea Time

William West is the unholy love child of William Gibson and Frank Zappa, a born and bred Ohio native transplanted to Reno, Nevada with a cat named Five. His shticks include writing, Perl programming, and teaching English as a second language. He enjoys empanadas, choripanes, completos, pizza, pirogies, pasta, potstickers, computery things, languages, telling his daughter stories on demand, and writing discomfiting fiction. His better half and little one currently reside in Santiago, Chile, and, if he ever gets his ever-loving stuff together, he'll be living there too.

Brandon Butler
All Aboard!

Brandon Butler is a Canadian and a Maritimer. Not necessarily in that order. Hailing from Halifax, Nova Scotia, he currently lives, works and writes from Toronto, Ontario. By day he toils as a computer programmer and by night... does the same. But also writes!

A previous second-place quarterly winner of the Writers of the Future Contest (Volume XIX), Brandon has just returned to writing after a 15 year hiatus. Welcome back. His latest work has been accepted for publication with Helios Quarterly Magazine, Third Flatiron Publishing and the forthcoming Monsters in Space anthology from Dragon's Roost Press.

Twitter: @2BWritingStuff

W. T. Paterson
Vlad's Incorruptible Soul

W. T. Paterson is the author of the novels DARK SATEL-LITES and WOTNA. A Pushcart Prize nominee and graduate of Second City Chicago, his work has appeared in over 50 publications worldwide, including Fiction Magazine, The Gateway Review, and The Paragon Press. A number of stories have been anthologized by Lycan Valley, North 2 South Press, and Thuggish Itch. He spends most nights yelling for his cat to "Get down from there!"

Brett Reistroffer

Editor

Brett Reistroffer is an editor and writer from the Pacific Northwest. He established Bad Dream Entertainment in 2013 as a home for dark, weird fiction from new and emerging voices in the worlds of horror, sci-fi, and fantasy.

Website: www.BrettReistroffer.com

Stefan Koidl

Cover Illustrator

Stefan Koidl is a full-time Krampus mask carver, self-taught illustrator, and concept artist living in Salzburg, Austria.

He started drawing when he was a little kid, fascinated with creating characters and scenes that don't exist in real life. Currently, Stefan specializes in digital paintings, and especially likes to paint creepy, dark stuff.

One of his biggest dreams is to be able to work as a full-time illustrator in the near future.

Website: www.artstation.com/stefankoidl
Facebook: www.facebook.com/The.Art.of.Stefan.Koidl
Instagram: www.instagram.com/stefankoidl

BAD DREAM ENTERTAINMENT

Dark Stories for Dark Minds

www.BadDreamEntertainment.com

www.Facebook.com/BadDreamEntertainment

www.Twitter.com/BadDreamPub